What You Wish For

Traveler Tales

ENRIQUE ARIZPE

Order this book online at www.trafford.com
or email orders@trafford.com

Most Trafford titles are also available at major online book retailers.

Printed in the United States of America.

ISBN: 978-1-4669-6527-0 (sc)
ISBN: 978-1-4669-6528-7 (e)

Trafford rev. 10/27/2012

 www.trafford.com

North America & international
toll-free: 1 888 232 4444 (USA & Canada)
phone: 250 383 6864 ✦ fax: 812 355 4082

Prologue

The Hero

Covered in sand, caked in sweat, staring at an evil doppelganger with bad hair, holding an unimaginably large cleaver-like sword. But I'm getting ahead of myself; the best way to begin is at my high school on the year of 2010. I was once again sulking in my English class while an unimaginably beautiful girl whom ignored me with an unnatural tenacity flirted with an ugly (in my opinion) guy. He was president of the student council obviously; my hateful thoughts against the weasel were melted away by the glorious laugh of the girl that resounded of angel song (also in my opinion). The following paragraph will be dedicated to describing this girl so skipping it will not be frowned upon.

She was a different kind of girl; she had a flower safely tucked within the halo of black hair that draped across her shoulders. Every day she seemed to concoct a new outfit to dazzle the public. Another exceptional ability of hers was how she grew exceedingly beautiful every time I saw her; unfortunately she also grew more and more ignorant of my affection and would forget who I was. The second half of this description will be coming soon, let's get back to the story.

As a freshman I floundered and failed to find a "home" among the throng of kids, I couldn't use the computer expertly, I was completely single, I wasn't very good at any sport other than soccer, I wasn't voted into student council, and the resident low-riders hated me with a passion, so I tried to sit at the same table as the girl of my dreams (the dreaded fresa table). The majority of my peers regarded me with equal indifference except the ones that disliked me. They ridiculed my very existence and utilized every moment they could obtain to make my life that much harder. I had attempted to sit with the beauties and they literally moved their table, leaving me pitifully alone.

I had spent much of the second half of my freshman year eating under a most depressing tree with very little shade and it was here that I plunged into a small bout of insanity. After I had regained my composure for social life I went to a nerdy table and I introduced them to trading card games. Other than dropping their overall GPA and draining them of their money as I sold them cards the table grew crowded. I had "befriended" a fellow by the name of Rob, he was slightly darker than I was and had a shaved head, he barked orders like a drill sergeant despite having no true influence on anyone. I proposed that we start our own table for cards; I didn't tell him of my scheme to insert my predestined table in the location with the best view, directly across from the aforementioned angel. As a side quest of sorts a homely ape of a freshman currently sat in this strategic spot. He hunched over the table in his mud green jacket munching on whatever mystery meat the school had decided to serve. As I sat at the table and settled in, pulled out my cards and put down my radio the goblinesque kid began to shudder and turned to me, "what are you doing?"

I smiled and flicked out a card, it glittered with foil, "playing Cards, wanna play?"

His dull eyes glittered at the sight of the card, and then he frowned, "I don't know how though," I taught him (his name was Joe) and every other misfit that drifted by my roaring table how to play. A colorful bunch of outcasts settled at my table, the first was Jacob, a large being with the cross-eyed face of a cat was one of them, but he didn't do much more than sleep. Rob had brought his own freshman whom looked just like him, only brighter. I found the duo strange because they both insisted on joining the marines. Not that there's anything wrong with it, it is an honorable and valiant occupation that if executed correctly will leave the hero scarred for life with hideous memories of death and sorrow. It may even give them the occasional horrific nightmare that awakes them in a cold sweat.

The table was ruled by both me and Rob and our kingdom had lasted several weeks before a disagreement on which of us the actual leader of the table was. It arose from my preference of the outer seat and refusal to let anyone else sit on my "throne." In the end we settled the dispute with a card game and I emerged victorious despite his cheating. With Rob gone more freshmen arrived, Noah was a very large freshman with matted hair that moved in as well as Orly, a thin lollipop headed kid. The final state of my empire had left me as the sole sophomore.

"Hippy King!" Joe would cry out every Friday during lunch. My name arose from my unique (in this region) hair, which curled around my head like the sun's corona. It was joined by my perfectly circular glasses and large nose which gave me the apparent appearance of a 60's rock band member that was shot by a crazed fan.

"My fresh minion!" I jovially bellowed as I would take my seat and whip out my radio and sandwich. I restrained a grin as I acted like I didn't know what day it was and then pull out the mat and specific cards for everyone to place their chips on. The freshman gathered around taking turns rolling dice and laughing in outrage as the beasts with their chips on them were defeated. This is how every day went at my table, the loudness and music and laughter (even the occasional sing along) it was great but I still felt a sense of something missing. The love of an angel. All of these things made up the basis of a relatively average life, but a story without a pinch of magic isn't a story worth reading, so that's where Djonie comes in.

CHAPTER 1

Bianca

After one day of lunch, my story officially begins, I went to my chemistry class where I sat next to the same breathtaking girl I'd been shamelessly tripping over, I couldn't help but notice that her long black hair was like a pluming forest that gave way to the barren and overly concealing shirt she wore. Although I could only see the side of her face her eyes still had a hypnotizing effect that could take the hardest of souls and melt them like a snowman in June. The rest of her face was splattered with freckles that only served to accentuate her beauty. The nose she possessed lacked any deformity and ended with the perfect angle, her faint eyebrows were the thin shade that draped over her powerful eyes, and her smile was a well sculpted crescent upon which a scimitar could be designed after. Her name was Bianca.

To my dismay she insisted on talking to the same political varmint that I had mentioned before. I requested to leave the classroom and go to the restroom, permission was granted and I dashed away. As I entered the lavatory I felt a fist of filth and funk smack me in the face, it was near unbearable and was on the verge of bringing tears to my eyes. Upon exiting the stall venturing to the sink I was baffled by an elaborately decorated pink bottle. On it was a crude carving of letters scarring the beautiful bottle:

PERFUME

I wanted to empty the bottle of its scent to combat the stench that surrounded me but I was suspicious. I had not heard anyone come in or out while I was here and I would have noticed this bottle when I had initially entered. I abandoned logic and sprayed the bottle hoping for relief when an even pinker plume of smoke drifted from the nozzle. I was enveloped in the choking smoke, the outline of a muscular man with a wisp where his feet should be floated into view. I could see the door out directly behind him.

It growled with a monstrous voice, "How do you do?" we were equally shocked by his voice. The creature twisted his beard as he cleared his throats in various tones and pitches, "my apologies," he squeaked, more twisting, "much better," his voice now sounded like a used car salesman. He was calm, "I am eternally grateful that you released me from that cramped bottle, my name is Djonie, in case you couldn't tell, I'm a genie."

He knew my next question, "no you don't get three wishes, that's a load of camel doo. You get one wish, no more, no less, and you can't wish for more wishes. So Russo, what do you want to wish for?"

I was cowering behind a trash can, "how do you know my name?"

"Is that a wish?"

"No."

"You're a clever one," Djonie scoffed, "you summoned me. Now are you gonna make a wish or am I gonna have to wait?" I simply turned my back to the phantasm, with that I left the restroom not actually believing that I had met a genie and ventured back to class and reached into my backpack and reached around. I was shocked to find the bottle. As I sat there ignoring the teacher's lecture and admiring Bianca from the corner of my eye I knew what I wanted. After class I went behind the school and summoned the genie, he came out with a clap of thunder and in a deep voice questioned, "Ready?" he grinned.

"I am, I've decided, I want Bianca to love me."

"What?" he smiled, "did I hear you correctly? You should know that as a genie I cannot grant such a wish, you must work for this prize, this is basic stuff, seriously," his grin was now spreading infectiously across his face revealing many teeth.

"Fine then, give me some kind of quest to have her, go ahead."

"Is this your wish? To have Bianca at any cost I propose?" he was now grinning so wide that an inch more would decapitate the apparition.

"Yes."

""Too easy!" he laughed as he snapped his fingers. Feeling your soul being ripped apart is a queer feeling, like swallowing a gallon of jelly and having it settle in the right ventricle of your heart. Then the jelly explodes and every pore on your body releases molten cheese. Then it feels as though your head is slammed into a brick wall made of feathers, it was almost but not entirely completely unlike death. The result was a clone of me, his nose was thinner, sideburns longer, and hair straight. His eyes had a distinct sunk in appearance to them, and he smirked. The genie and imposter puffed away as I looked around me at the smoldering wreckage. My lungs stung with smoke. The school was gone, or at least, not here anymore.

I looked to the edge of the piece of earth I floated on. Below me was the school, and I could see parts of it phase into existence next to the shard I stood on until the entire structure had been redesigned for Djonie's purpose. Hallways curled in and out stretched ridiculously to floating rooms and patios. All of the halls led to the newly shaped cafeteria which was now wider and roared with the fanfare of a coliseum. The new structure was inhabited by strange blue liquid filled membranes that drifted from place to place like sentient jellyfish. They were mostly transparent and a simple heart and brain were floating within the blue substance, instead of legs I noticed that they had primitive tentacles. They didn't seem too intelligent but they seemed to have an air of importance, they were probably a very rich species. As my vision focused better I saw that beyond the floating segments of earth and jelly people was a wall of whirling wind, we seemed to be protected and held aloft by the oversized twister.

As I reached the cafeteria I saw it was indeed a coliseum. Within I saw Djonie twisting his beard in various directions, beside him was my copy, "Welcome," Djonie echoed as though from a microphone, "to the Tournament of Smashing Praise! My name is Djonie and I'll be your host for the duration of this game. The lucky gladiator to defeat each of his opponents will have one rule free wish!" he paused and my thoughts immediately turned to the voluptuous Bianca, "all that is required to enter this arena is a raise of the hand," the sight of hands pushing out of the stands and reaching for the strangely yellow sky shocked me, I hadn't realized that my hand had rose as well. Djonie snapped his finger and there was a flash of light.

Clouds drifted in and out of my view, when I was able to turn my head I realized that there was a screen that showed my body pixilated and blank. As I tried to wrench myself from the bed I was attached to Djonie materialized, "heya champ," he had a Brooklyn accent, "I'm gonna make you the greatest fighta ever! But first we gotta get you a fighting name, how about the Flaming Petunia?"

"What?"

"Good point, might not sit well with the public," Djonie pretended to muse, "we should probably get you a weapon and suit first." He began to type a series of codes into the screen.

"Why am I tied to this wall?" I questioned

"So the suit gets your exact shape and doesn't accidentally stitch itself into your skin," Djonie casually replied in his "normal" voice. I sat patiently as he began to bring up a variety of available costumes.

"Why do I need a costume anyways?"

"Have you ever been to Atlantis?"

"No."

"Then that analogy won't work, how about a wrestling match?"

"I've seen 'em before," I replied

"Okay then, you see this is a show, I'm making big bucks off of those rich water sacs and they want a flashy show. The way this game works is that its single elimination, if you are defeated you are immediately teleported to the home-pod, where you will be kept in stasis until the end of the tournament. Most of the matches will have the objective of cutting down your opponent gladiator style," he paused and waved his hand over the screen, "but remember that no matter how badly they seem to be defeated they aren't actually dead, they're sent away, but for the sake of the show, you should act like every severance and mutilation is as real as this entire wish," he smiled a sinister look, "I think I found your outfit."

I looked at the screen, "Does it come in red?"

The resulting garb was comprised of a red hood sewn onto a maroon tunic. The tunic had thin sleeves that tapered outward to give considerable wrist room. The Tunic went down to my knees; below it was a simple pair of cargo shorts. I was given a pair of death black sneakers to go with the costume. Djonie happily gave me a weapon he felt would go well with my costume. It was a simply built sickle with an elongated handle. Djonie then bellowed, "Your name will be the Red Reaper!" He then allowed me to be released by the platform, gave me a foreboding wink, and snapped his fingers; I was now alone in a large auditorium.

The floor was made of marble and the ceiling was comprised of velvet. The walls were smothered in a variety of paintings depicting wars I had never seen or dreamt of. I felt the weight of my weapon in a holster stitched to the back of my uniform. I withdrew it by wrapping a black glove around the blade and pulling it up. I slid it back in and practiced multiple times to see how fast I could do it. After I thought I had gotten the hang of it I began to swing my flimsy weapon around clanging it against the marble statues all around me. My footsteps echoed loudly as the marble began to crumble under the blade I held. I glanced to the lone, yet ridiculously large window, the greenish sun was setting, I must've practicing for a pretty long time.

It took me awhile to notice that I was being watched, she looked familiar but I didn't know her name. I realized that she obviously had no idea who I was due to the hood that concealed my face. As I attempted to approach her she quickly fled into the darkness, so I pursued her. I followed her to a well lit room but slightly less ornate than velvet and marble rooms. It was stone gray and reeked of processed meat. A variety of people sat at several bland tables. I decided that because I had a new identity I would start off big, I sat with the burliest, biggest, bunch of brutes I could find. Unfortunately they picked up the table and moved off; I sat with my tray on my knees and ate alone. I looked to the center and saw a sickly, sniveling sliver of a human. He had a pathetic monkey mask on that failed to hide his uneven teeth, I couldn't help but laugh, "Joe?"

"How do you know my name," he growled as I saw a blade slip from his sleeve to his hand.

"I should know the name of my fresh minions! Why don't you recognize me, oh yeah," I took off my hood, "how 'bout now?"

"Hippy King!" he screeched as he put away his weapon.

"They call me the Red Reaper, what's your 'name'?"

"I'm the Flaming Pancake of Doom! Wait a minute, I thought you hated fighting. What would you wish for?"

"do you see that girl over there," I briefly nodded to Bianca's seat at the adjacent table, "I love her and I will use this prize the genie is giving to win her over."

"You've had some pretty farfetched schemes before but this is insane," Joe replied, "have you seen the size of some of these guys?"

"Yeah, and it makes me suspicious," I confessed.

"Why?"

"I've never seen some of these fighters and I'm pretty sure they're fake or working for Djonie. He doesn't want to make it easy for me to win."

Joe seemed confused, "you make it sound like Djonie is personally trying to stop you." I didn't have a chance to reply to Joe's comment because a large billboard that took up the back wall began to glow and announced the two fighters to enter the next match:

ROUND 4
RED REAPER
VS.
SKIPPER

My skin felt odd as I realized that I was beginning to be teleported to the ring, the streaks of yellow left my eyes and I saw that I was in a pit of sand and that across from me was my opponent. He was clad in pale blue porcelain and held a black halberd with a green ribbon tied to it. I wore a steel looking skull mask that was met at the top by a cap that made the mask seem angry. He had two shoulder pads, one of which had a boar's head sculpted onto it. In short he looked like a deadly hockey player. I was shocked by the speed with which the brute charged me, boar head first halberd ready to skewer me. I suffered a glance to the stands and saw Bianca watching the match, I charged the hulk without my weapon with my black clad hands out wide, yelling.

As Skipper attempted to stab me with his weapon I grabbed it and pushed it down and used it as a kind of lever to propel me higher than my opponent, I then whipped out my sickle and hooked my blade beneath his mask, I yanked on my blade in midair and was pulled toward my opponent as his mask unhinged and the bottom half cracked. His face was young beneath the shattered mask and I hesitated during my next move, the young fighter charged once again but I simply ducked. The dangerous bit of the blade had passed and I gripped the ribbon he had. A quick yank robbed my opponent of his blade. Skipper was now standing still, bewildered by his loss of a weapon, he was stunned. I walked to my opponent and asked him to please forfeit. He tore off what remained of his mask and I saw that he was in fact a computer nerd that I had sold cards to in the past. He growled a very mean word followed by "you" and attempted to charge me.

I grabbed his decorated shoulder and ripped off the boar, I proceeded to punch the porcelain chest plate in. I hooked his foot with my sickle and flipped him onto his back, "Forfeit." He obliged and was teleported to what I assumed to be a safer spot.

CHAPTER 2

Ann

The next day was stormy outside but like always I sat at the table with Joe. We wondered where the rest of our gang was, if they had managed to make it past the preliminary round that is. As if on cue a large warrior in a latex yellow cat suit with nine tails flapping walked over to me. I knew it was Jacob, "don't you think that's a little tight?" Jacob just laughed and danced.

The reunion was cut short as Joe burrowed beneath the table and whispered, "Girl at twelve O' clock!" I turned to see the same girl that had seen me train; I ignored the sound of the crash as Jacob tripped on one of his tails and knocked over the table.

I greeted her kindly and she gave me a distracted, "hello," I looked to the area her eyes uneasily sat and saw Joe with his mouth agape; he was apparently fixated on our guests chest.

I subtly rammed the handle of my sickle into his shin and hissed, "Joe, it's impolite to stare."

"I wasn't staring," he weakly protested and continued to look at her.

"Pardon my comrades," I said, "they aren't the best trained bunch, my name is Ru-, er, my name is Red." She was attractive it was true; she had a certain cuteness to her that Bianca lacked. Her lips were well designed and full while her eyes were an agreeable shade with comfortable gaze. Her hair glimmered red at some points where the light hit it right. I took the moment to ask her what her name is.

"My name is Ann," my friends and I were wondering if you would like to sit with us," this was what broke Joe's shameless concentration, "just you though," she quickly added.

I had a choice, I could honor my friends, or I could go sit with a slew of girls. I knew what Joe and Jacob would do, but I couldn't abandon them; I smiled a wide grin and replied with a heavy hearted "No. But you can bring your friends over here."

She walked away while Jacob and Joe admired her back side, commenting on its width and fullness. I sat back in my seat with a half grin and began to realize something was missing. I couldn't find my sandwich and turned to the two dunces, "have you guys seen my sandwich?"

A lollipop headed being wearing a potato sack over his head with three holes held my sandwich, he also had my sickle. The rest of his suit was simple, just blue jeans and a sweater. I knew it was Orly, he had apparently found out who I was. I simply sipped some of my tea, "give them back Orly."

"No," he laughed, "and my name is the Thief."

"Why?"

"That's what the genie named me."

"Not that," I snapped, "why can't I have my sandwich?"

"Oh, that's because you have to catch me first!" he dashed off, I didn't bother to chase him, and he'd come back when he got bored but the board already displayed the next match:

ROUND 130
FISHY FLIER
VS.
RED REAPER

I saw the same sparks again as I was brought to the gate entering the ring. A strange voice which I assumed to be Djonie's announced the two fighters and as my introduction came to conclusion the door opened and I stepped onto the muddy battle ground. I reached for my sickle and felt a deep set fear in my gut. Orly had my weapon. It continued to rain as I saw the Flier come into view behind the haze. She had a long three pronged chain that she swung around herself. She wasted no time to fling the hook at me, and immediately began to reel it back in after I dodged it.

Her appearance was less than intimidating; she was a scrawny little fighter with a yellow moon mask concealing half her face, the other side was exposed but lacked emotion. My opponent danced along the muck throwing her blade every way she wanted, occasionally latching onto my tunic and ripping away fabric. The crowd was displeased with how I ran, but I didn't care enough to try and fight back yet. This continued until her hook had been momentarily stuck in the mud as she threw it slightly lower. She took a few seconds to reel it back in.

Then all I had to do was trick the Flier into sticking her hook into the mud, but I couldn't concentrate on a fool proof strategy or any strategy at all. I just kept running around hoping that chance would make it happen. Soon I heard the glorious sound of mud splattering and clinging to her hook. I stepped onto the blade to drive it deeper and ran over to the Fishy Flier. I planted one strong punch on her small face and knocked her out. I stood above her unconscious husk dripping with sweat and rain, panting. I had won, but I felt bad about it.

I was teleported away to the exit. I was greeted by Ann and Joe whom helped me get to my room; I hadn't noticed the wound I had received. The bone on my left knee was exposed and slightly chipped, it hurt immensely but I didn't want Ann to see that. I requested Ann find a bandage to wrap the damage to stop the seemingly endless bleeding. Once Ann was back and helping me with the bandaging Joe pulled my sickle from nowhere in particular, "I got it back from Orly, but it didn't seem like you needed it."

"It was luck," I replied.

"Sure, punching that guy out with one swift movement was luck, it was amazing, you could be one of those famous guys with moves like that, and you could have your own cereal!"

"Right, anyways," I replied to Joe's rambling, "how was your match?"

"Ooh it was easy I caught the guy on fire!"

"Isn't that a bit gruesome?"

"Nope, see ya!" and Joe was off.

After a few seconds of walking with Ann I asked what she thought of the match. "You were very lucky," she answered.

"I feared for my life," I said.

"I'm sure you'll do fine, I know that you can do it," she smiled. I simply smiled back.

When I had reached my room I turned to her and paused for a quick second to decide to tell her, "Thanks, I guess I'll see you tomorrow," I shrugged and closed the door; she had a disappointed face for some reason.

I stood in the darkness for a few minutes, after every match I always had a bad feeling. I almost always felt like emptying my stomach of whatever I had eaten that day and collapsing. I steadied myself attempting to focus on the sliver of pseudo-moon light in my window. After feeling like I couldn't go through with the tournament I'd force myself to rationalize that it was just a game and that Djonie said no one would get hurt. I plopped onto my bed, the fake alien moon cast a white glow onto me, and I hung my sickle beside my bed before drifting off to sleep.

I'm at a Pagoda of some sort, wooden bridges going to and fro while a murky dark green liquid flows beneath them. Fog encompasses the entire area, yet the bridges maintain their intense red, all of the features of this place are exaggerated, the bridges have extreme arcs that vary from spot to spot. I walk along the bridges slowly at first, searching for someone. My legs pick up speed as I begin to move quicker, I am now running across the bridges in a fit of irrational fear. I slip off the bridge and stumble into the liquid that was water, though extremely warm. As I drift below the murky depths I lose my sense of direction and attempt to swim although I may be going deeper into the shadow. I feel stiff now and feel sharp pains in my back and chest, ahead of me I see a large skeletal fish charge me with a full set of teeth spread wide to swallow me.

The sunlight was shining through the window when I awoke and patted myself all over to ensure that I remained in one piece. I dressed into my costume, which was oddly sewn up, and left for the mess hall for lunch. Joe was happily vibrating in his seat. "Hippy, I have some amazing news!"

"What?"

"We have our own trading cards! See?" Joe held up four packages with four pictures of fighters with their names stylishly plastered onto them. The first was the Blue Brawler, my doppelganger stood with his arms cross and horned mask sculpted from what seemed like mercury shining. The second had a brooding figure named Epoch, he had a complexly designed staff with a skeleton tied to it. The next one was a large being named Han, he wore both a boxer's shorts and wrestler's mask, not much else could cover his boulder like body. The last showed a person dressed as Robin Hood. He had a yellow feather in his fedora hat. His dark green mask concealed who he was but his bug-eyes were still visible. He had many bony features to his face and a twisted grin. He held a bow and arrow and was aiming intently at an object not on the wrapping. He was called the Unstrung Aero.

I knew the whole point of the cards was to line Djonie's pockets (if he has pockets) with our money. The cards were insanely expensive and mostly the same. Djonie was obviously enjoying the manufacture of these cards.

My card was red and depicted me happily bashing the Fishy Flier's face in with a maniacal grin painted onto my face. The name Red Reaper was typed out in the corner in white letters and there were numbers scattered across it that pertained to game play. I was a rare. Joe frowned as he found his early on through our pack popping and discovered he was merely a common. I was subtly pleased.

I was also pleased to discover that only some days would have matches to give each warrior time to rest. I had already spent two days with those blasted cards and I wanted the third day to be something fun since I would have a match the next day. Ann said that she had a surprise for me.

She and I ate with two of her friends, one of whom was Bianca; the other was a girl by the name of Pearl. Pearl was equally attractive to both of her friends. She had long, curly brown hair that seemed very soft. Her face was wider than Ann's and had a thin, wide smile that was perpetually painted on. Her body was thinner than the other two already thin beauties. Her eyes were as dark as mine and she seemed to enjoy my every bad pun. She simply had the appearance of a sculpture sculpted by Donatello himself. I had a feeling that I may have chosen the wrong girl for a crush. But if I had, I didn't know who I should've chosen.

I tried very hard to enjoy myself but Bianca made me nervous and I couldn't shake the feeling that I was being a nuisance to the group of girls, I felt more unwanted than usual. I ate very little and frequently left to go to the restroom, but all I did was stand in the mirror and tell myself to go back. I could tell that Ann was worried about me and Pearl was curious as to why I left every few minutes. Bianca was amused with my plight. One last stare at the mirror and I was ready, I was going to tell Bianca exactly what I felt. I marched out of the john and to their table. I saw that Pearl had left and had been replaced by two fighters. Bianca was giggling and sitting on one of their laps while the other one was running his fingers through Ann's hair, she didn't seem too happy.

I approached the table and was greeted with less than friendly words from the fighters. I politely asked the brute to stop fondling Ann's hair. He rose from his seat, he was slightly shorter than me but his green hat and feather made up the distance, and demanded that I ask him again. I did and I felt a swift pain in my gut afterward. He laughed, "Do you realize who I am? I'm the Unstrung Aero. I do as I please, besides she was having a good time, weren't you Fran?"

"Her name is Ann," I grunted.

"Do you think I care? Look, I'm the best fighter there is, you should watch one of my matches, even though it only takes a few seconds. I might even have to cut you down someday. Trust me there's a reason everybody loves me!" he cackled, "You see, being the hero has its upsides, especially when you don't have to worry about any actual monsters. You have had it easy no doubt; I always have to be in the last rounds. Regardless I think you should leave, unless you want me and my buddy to make you leave."

I reached for the sickle in its holster and was stopped by the crossbow in Aero's hand. The point was pulled back directly in front of my face, my hand relaxed and I looked behind him at Bianca. Aero laughed again and tried to pull back my hood, "Let's see the peasant behind this mask," he spat before Ann stood up and put her hand on his shoulder, she whispered something in his ear. He put down the weapon and looked back at Bianca, "really?" he had a not too innocent grin. She nodded and he dashed across the table to greet her.

I exhaled as I looked at her, "thank you."

"What else are friends for?" she smiled. I walked her to her room before the night fell on us. She invited me in and I obliged. She had a much nicer room with a wide variety of small statues and paintings. She pulled out a dark brown hunk of bread shaped like an oversized donut. She told me it was a spice cake. My stomach gladly accepted her generous gift; it was possibly the best thing to ever grace my taste buds. I voiced my love for her cake and she merely laughed, "thank you."

I lightly glided to my room and crawled into my bed. For once I couldn't decide who it was I would rather have with me. I felt good to be uncertain and not care so much for once.

Plains spread all around me, the shadows of the clouds gliding across the earth, I feel myself yell something but I can't hear it. There is no sound at all. I walk for what seems an eternity without the sound but soon I reach a strange break in the plains. A bright white light severs the expanse, the other side lacked anything, and I could see nothing past the light. I pass the boundary and a flood of sounds bombard my ears, but I see nothing. I now walk blindly through the perpetual shadows and use my ears to hear the sound of the wind cutting through the blades of grass.

I reach a vortex of sorts composed of sound and fall into it. The sun that belongs to Earth shines brightly beneath my feet and I can hear the sound of waves crashing on stones. As I land on the sun I feel that it is actually very cold. I walk over to a small hut and walk into it. It is featureless save for a queen sized bed. I can see Bianca beneath the covers. Beside her is the Aero, he opens his eyes at me and smiles. He pulls a crossbow out from under the sheets and points it at me, "I win."

CHAPTER 3

Pearl

I was very tired the next day and incredibly irritable. Joe was especially annoying. As a result I insulted him whenever the chance arose until his anger rose to meet mine. The hostility between us was reaching a high point and I couldn't wait to go to today's match to try and vent my frustration on my opponent. A sick feeling slipped into my gut as I gazed at the cruel screen:

ROUND 193
FLAMING PANCAKE OF DOOM
VS.
RED REAPER

Joe had a grim smile on his face, his mask quivered with excitement, I had always known about Joe's explosive temper though never seen it. I had a feeling that it was going to be quite the show. We were both teleported away to our starting positions. I stepped out with the green sun above me casting my suit in an orange glow. A dagger dashed past me into the shadows. I acted as though it had hit me and watched as Joe gleefully sprinted to my side. Joe was ecstatic while he placed a small and sticky explosive device to my back. He leaned over to me before activating it, "you have thirty seconds to live."

Orly and Ann anxiously watched the ordeal as I knew it would end. Joe began to flee the blast radius but failed to notice that I had slipped the sticky bomb into his shorts. The ensuing explosion was gruesomely loud and the pained yelp that rose from Joe was haunting. I luckily did not hear it; I had begun to walk away from the ring as soon as he ran to what he had sadly believed to be a safe spot. I did not speak to anyone as I sulkily slinked into my bed. I laid in there attempting to rationalize what I had just done, there was no right reason for killing my friend. How could any of these "combatants" bring themselves to destroy others, how could so many of us willingly join these gruesome games? These dreadful thoughts swirled around me as I slipped into somber sleep.

It was summer, I was home and happy. My dad was cooking out and the smell of fajitas was drifting through the air. The plate was set in front of me and I happily ate. But as I bit into the meat my mouth went numb and I was in great pain, my arm bled out onto the fresh green grass staining it an unearthly red. My arm fell to the ground and squirmed around before leaping for my throat pinning me to the ground.

I spent most of the following days alone, Ann didn't look at me and every one else avoided me at all costs. Djonie had capitalized what had happened and portrayed me as a ruthless cut throat that would annihilate anyone that stood in my way. I was quickly labeled as the villain despite equally terrifying acts, such as the Aero's ruthless victories. I had felt bad enough, and then I saw the next wave of warrior cards. There was a Rare named Red, The Reaper of the Weak. I hated it all.

I wanted to escape the world Djonie had designed for me, this was my own wish turned in upon itself. I began to move away from the main grounds, as close to the vortex barrier as I could, to an oddly convenient clearing in a strangely placed forest. I yelled out Djonie's name in the middle of the clearing certain it would go unnoticed.

"Yes?" he smiled in his rich guy accent. He wore a well padded business suit and large brimmed hat with a pink feather. His fingers were covered in rings of varying precious metals and stones, "I've heard about your last riveting match, congratulations!"

Trying to hide my surprise at the genie's appearance I hardened my face, "I hate you," I had never said those words to anyone. The clearing had taken a dark purplish hue and the green star that gave this world heat was veiled over.

"No you don't, you love this, think of all the fame you are receiving!"

"You mean infamy."

"They are the same; I'm just exploiting your bad boy image kid. You'll be the big bad wolf that the more sympathetic viewers will root for."

I paused, "did you say 'viewers'?"

"Of course, why would I limit myself to mere coliseum matches, people come from all over Valhalla just to see my show, so I simply publicize it, more and more money pours in, its genius."

"You selfish, see through, piece of-"

"You sound upset," Djonie laughed, "don't act like you don't enjoy crushing your opponents."

"I don't enjoy it, I can't. To be honest I can't feel at all. All I feel is hatred toward you."

Djonie glowed purple, "I've given you a chance at love and you have hate? What about those three girls? Or would you rather I get rid of them?"

"Listen you bag of smoke and mirrors, stay away from them!"

"Firstly, you have some terrible insults. You should work on those, secondly, it would seem I've struck a nerve, which one is it?" he chuckled grimly. He began to laugh louder, I grew much madder and in a burst of rage raised my sickle and sliced down on him, he stopped laughing. His face was twisted into a sadistic smile, "ouch," he grinned before turning a deep green, "Well then! I guess it's time to kick things up a notch!" He snapped his fingers and popped out of the room.

I went back to my room; someone had spray-painted a less than kind phrase on to my door and left whatever mystery meat the Mess had left smeared across the door hinges and knob. The food had hardened to a near brick like state and froze the door in place (it has that effect on the colon too). I tried to pry open the crusty door but it was stuck. I leaned against my door and put my sickle down. It was now very dark, there were no lights of any kind beside the fake moon, and I knew that no one would take me in, Joe was gone, and Ann was afraid of me. Orly didn't trust me, Jacob didn't either, I didn't know Pearl well enough and I couldn't even attempt to talk to Bianca.

I walked quite far through the halls and courtyards of the realm. Just as I had predicted no one would let me in, except for Pearl, she was understanding of my plight and allowed me to sleep on her floor. Despite the primitive accommodations I was grateful. The cold hard ground was actually very comfortable. I passed out quite quickly.

The pagoda I had seen before was now foggier than before, I was drenched and gasping for air. A dead skeletal fish was flopping beside me. I stood up and felt irritably cold. A warm flame sat on a ledge only a few meters away. As I attempted to put my left foot forward I realized that it was very light, very short, and very bloody. I fell to the ground, and without the aid of my legs crawled to the ledge.

The flame was surrounded by two rings of water floating around it. The ball of flame levitated and its appearance resembled that of an atom. I felt myself drifting toward the nucleus of the flame and soon reached the sphere. The heat seared my skin and bleached my hair; the scent of burning flesh filled the air. Calmness consumed me as my vision turned white.

Pearl woke me up with the smell of something I remembered fondly, spice cake. Pearl smiled with her full set of perfectly aligned teeth and said, "I told Ann that I let you stay over so she sent me this cake. She said you'd like it," The rags I had slept with had not hit the ground before I had reached the table and munched down on the first slice, she laughed, it was a nice sound, "why weren't you able to stay at your place?"

"Someone sealed it with slimy cafeteria food."

"It sounds like somebody doesn't like you."

"Somebody?" I spat with fragments of cake in my mouth, "in case you haven't heard, I am the single most hated warrior in the realm! I was surprised you would let me in what with the propaganda that the genie has been spewing across the air waves."

"Propaganda?" was all she could squeak.

"Have you seen the slogans to some of these products? Like Djonie's Alarm System: 'so good Red'll stay out of your house and the neighbors'!', or how about the Champion's Sport Drink? They say that it's good because the Reaper won't drink it."

Pearl was smiling, "why does that matter?"

I paused and thought about it, it didn't matter. I suddenly felt much better about myself, and liked her much more than when I had entered her dorm the night before. I looked up at her from my food, I looked at her eyes. They were darker then I remembered. They were alluring, sensual even, I felt myself leaning closer to her. My breath was caught in my throat as I realized just how close I was, she didn't seem to mind but I felt extremely uncomfortable and intrusive. I barely knew her but I could feel something within me continued to pull me toward her.

The two of us happily walked over to the mess hall laughing at my jokes. Orly quickly ran over to me, "Russo, the first match is about to be announced!"

"I'm glad I already ate!" I said to Pearl as I looked up at the board:

ROUND 225
RED REAPER
VS.
SPIDER-MONKEY

I happily bowed as I felt the teleportation take place. The opponent before me had a strange get up entirely comprised of what seemed to be clunky iron plates and furry monkey hair over the shoulders and joints as well as a life-like tail. He had no weapon besides long yellowish fingernails. I felt almost sorry for him as I swung my sickle down onto the little beast's head.

A loud clang and a series of sharp pains in my chest followed the attack. It took me a moment to realize that the cretin was clamped around my neck and clawing at my face. His nails drove into my cheeks and forehead cleaving the skin off of it. I screamed and felt small tears well up in my eyes as I dove into the mud monkey first and stunned the monster.

My sickle successfully missed the creature as it slid off his armor. I decided to hack away the edges of its armor through the hairy patches on its joints. It was much more difficult than I had expected due to the fact that bits of skin and blood drooped off of my face onto my eyes. But soon I had its chest exposed and was horrified to discover that the metal plating had been its chest. It no longer moved and the primitive organs were left out in the open as I lost my spice cake all over the sandy floor.

I made my way back to the mess hall. Once there I saw that Orly had removed his mask, he seemed upset. When I asked him what was wrong he simply replied, "I've been disqualified."

"What?"

Ann walked over to us, "he's been accused of stealing some very important information from the staff."

Ann refrained from cringing as she carefully wrapped up my mangled face, ironically she still could not tell who I was. She had Orly and Pearl obtain a variety of ointments to fix the scarring, it was at this point that I asked her, "how do you know such effective healing methods?"

She frowned, "I thought you knew, I haven't the slightest clue what I'm doing, I'm actually guessing."

This was not comforting. I looked up to the battle board to see who was next, Orly's name had been covered by a large red X and my name was typed in above it. They were going to force me into another match. I checked the opponent:

ROUND 234
RED REAPER

VS.
HAN

I put my head down and pulled my hood over my head, Ann pulled up my chin and looked at me, "You can do this," Pearl nodded in agreement. Orly grinned and Jacob was asleep as I felt the teleportation take effect. They seemed to have forgotten my apparent villainy if only for the moment.

The rush of cool wind swept around me before being replaced with the green sun's blistering heat. The large being named Han lumbered before me, he did not come out of a door like most fighters, he was instead lowered by a machine that somewhat resembled a thundercloud. It was the brute that I had seen on the card packs, but he was unnaturally large, the last monstrosity I had fought was an actual spider/monkey so I believed it possible that Djonie had created this beast as well. He was huge, imagine a large man for a moment, no bigger, you're getting there, visualize a young blue whale, that's a good size comparison. His muscles were each the size of a youth in the fetal position and it seemed as if a mere flex could snap his miniscule head off its shoulders. So to put is shortly: he was big and Djonie didn't want me to win.

Before I could even reach for my sickle he had me in his grasp. He squeezed tightly and I felt every joint in my body, even some I didn't know I had, pop. The monster then began his rampage through the town surrounding us. He seemed to be more of an oversized toddler as opposed to a menacing thug. I could simply trick him, and maybe then gain the upper hand.

He happily chortled and squeezed harder, I felt a rib snap as I began my plea, "wait, you don't understand," I could taste blood, "I'm supposed to win, I'm the good guy," I felt his grip loosen, I took this opportunity to slide my arm across my shattered side to my weapon, I began to rub the blade against his finger.

"Story?" said the thoughtless dullard.

"Yes, I have to live; otherwise the story comes to a conclusion."

"Am I in your1 story?" he asked in a truly childish way.

"Of course you are, do you want to know what happens next?" I spat out a glob of blood.

"Yes!" his grip tightened with excitement.

"You put me down," at which point I severed his large pinky, he bled a watery substance, I knew it wasn't real! Djonie's construct wailed in realistic pain and stomped around as he dropped me a great distance, my fall was broken by the severed pinky and I landed with a light yet painful thump. Strangely enough the match did not end when he crashed through the boundaries of the city Djonie had designed. I attempted to limp after the juggernaut but my injuries were too extensive, I collapsed into the rubble unable to focus my thoughts.

A smaller version of Han's cloud machine hovered over me and lifted me into it. The interior was dark and illuminated by a single light in the center. The control panel cast a dim light on the lollipop headed pilot. I could feel myself grow weak, then an individual with long curly hair drifted into my sight, she held what looked like a wrench of some sort. She went out of sight and I could feel several cold plates cover my most extensive injuries. After a short period of time as I nodded in and out of consciousness I felt much better and was able to lift my head and see myself on a monitor.

I was swinging from building to building with my sickle and plowing through Han's attacks with ease; I was nimble and graceful and with one stroke decapitated the brute, blue ooze spewed in all directions. I felt very good about myself until I realized that I was still in the cloud machine. I had grown very tired and looked closely at the imposter and saw a slight bulge in its chest, the rest of her body was slender and well designed, "Ann?" I was very tired but would not rest. I sat up in the bed of the chamber and demanded to know what was happening.

Pearl was smiling, "you need to rest, your matches are being played by Ann. Just rest."

"You mean that she is wearing my suit?" I felt my face and was stopped by the bandages, but they felt fresh, as if they'd been unwrapped and replaced by better ones, "You didn't see anything did you?"

"Yes I did, and I couldn't believe how big it was," she smiled wider as she placed a gentle hand on my leg.

"What?" I said rising from my bed with painful speed.

"Your nose," she said confused.

"You saw my face?" I had no reason to be but I was actually kind of alarmed.

"No one else knows other than me, Ann, Orly, and that cat guy." She later explained that Orly had stolen this very contraption as well as the plates that accelerate healing she had placed on me. It was because of these very items that he had been disqualified. I was grateful for such useful allies; Ann later came up into the cloud and was happy to see me awake.

I thanked Ann for taking my place and involuntarily rubbed my face, Orly looked back from the pilot's seat and taunted, "She won't be taking all of your matches, after the next fight you have to get back in the saddle."

I turned my attention to the screen and saw Jacob plop onto the stage, "Who's he going up against?" I called out.

"The Unstrung Aero," the group said in solemn unison, my stomach turned. Jacob had only stepped onto the sand when a terrible twang filled the air. Apparently every match was always the same, a foolish challenger approaches the proud and charming Aero, Aero replies with a blue arrow that rings like a cobra's hiss through the battlefield. The bolt punctures the base of the neck and sends its host flying back into the shadows; he would then come out into the light and bow giving an "inspirational" speech for the "good" guys everywhere. This time he just pulled out an arrow with a cord tied to it and shot it into the crowd. The arrow struck no one but firmly planted into the seat beside Bianca. She happily slid down it and into his arms, she gave him a long hug and lacerating kiss before the camera zoomed in on his face, "This one's for the Red Reaper, your foul reign will soon end and you will have to answer to my shaft!" Orly was laughing as the Aero shot an arrow into the cloud above and carried Bianca up into it with him.

I really disliked that guy for painfully obvious reasons. I asked no one in particular, "does he always get a one shot kill?"

"Yup," Orly replied, "but don't worry they say that a true warrior can dodge the first volley so that won't be too difficult for you."

"They also say," continued Pearl, "that only a true heart can dodge his second strike."

"His third attack," Ann interjected, "can be avoided only by one with a true purpose. If you can pull all of this off you probably can beat him."

I let out a long sigh. Pearl sprung to my side telling me to lie down to avoid my bones from healing crooked. I passed out into a calm rest.

The land was choked by fog. As far as I could tell, the ground was covered in wilted flowers of some sort. Every step crunched loudly and echoed off of the mists. I tried to focus on what was in front of me, moving much quicker than I was. It was a large hulk of metal; two large horns adorned its forehead vertically. It had no eyes that I could see and several spikes jutted from odd angles on its body. I noticed that it lacked arms and legs instead jerking in a spastic manor with the spikes below it.

It was now meters away and I could hear the clockwork within grinding angrily. I could not get away, the crushed flowers had turned into vines and wrapped around my legs, I had no choice but to take the impact. The result left my body impaled on the variety of spikes which now rotated and shook tearing the remains apart, it was gruesome to say the least but I felt that I was finally safe once it flung me to the ground. Then it turned and charged me again.

I awoke to see Pearl sleeping by my side, she was quite beautiful in the dim light and it took my mind off the healing bones. I lied on the bed for an extended amount of time before actually rising. Once I had Orly let out a strained laugh, "it's about time, first you were in a week long coma and then you spent an hour staring at Pearl, you've more patience than I do!"

Chapter 4

Mishrel

I was now much better and it just so happened that Orly had managed to hack into the program that could control the order of the matches. He then extracted my list and determined that I would be matched up against five more opponents, in what should only be three. He turned to me, "Could you go find Ann for me? I'm hungry and her spice cake sounds delicious, in the meantime I took the liberty of reducing your matches to the three mandatory matches, your next one will be later today against Epoch. Later this week will be some guy named Mr. M and then the semifinals will have you fighting the Unstrung Aero."

I nodded and turned to Pearl's sleeping form, I tapped her shoulder. She groggily awoke and looked around. She brightened as she saw my face; I had forgotten that I still did not have my suit. I invited her to help me find Ann. The two of us happily walked through the iron halls of the stolen cloud. A cold draft flowed through the halls that chilled me severely. Pearl rubbed her arms; I turned to her, "are you cold?" I asked in a gentlemanly manner.

"Yeah," she said, her breath was visible.

"You know we can stay warm easier if we share body heat, so if we walk close to each other it should keep us pretty warm," I wasn't sure if she'd say yes but I really wanted her to.

She nodded and came very close to me. Her perfume smelled tangy and sweet and her hair fell from her shoulders to meet her chest. I wrapped an arm around her as we walked. She was considerably warm. I could feel my heart beat in my chest as we continued to walk, it matched hers. She was getting warmer and warmer, and the two of us continued to get closer than before. I felt extremely relaxed and we barely spoke. It was perfect until we actually found Ann.

She had been working in the kitchen and making all kinds of pastries. I sampled one considerably amazing muffin; it left a zing to the taste buds that lasted a good amount of time. I complemented the culinary wizard on her job well done and informed her of Orly's request for a spice cake. Ann simply reached into her oven and pulled out a fresh cake. She stepped onto a simple elevator and was lifted to the bridge.

Pearl and I stood in the much warmer kitchen amongst the baked goods. She took a step towards me, her eyes fixed on mine. I took a step forward as well, our noses were within bumping distance, but before I could finally have my first kiss I was teleported to a changing room. My racing mind was confused as I felt my casual layers of clothing removed by mechanical arms and my hooded tunic and sickle were given to me. I was again teleported to the battlefield in a match against the apparent Epoch. He had taken the design for my reaper costume, complete hood and cloak covered in tatters and tears, only black. He had a gnarled stick with a skull impaled onto it where the scythe's blade would be. The skull was sewn into the rest of the bones with intestine of some kind. The skeleton lacked hands and feet instead the stumps were sharpened to act as a weapon. He was called a master of illusion by some though I had yet to know why.

His weapon clicked and clacked as he began to advance slowly. His pale skin hung to his malnourished frame and his chin had three sprouting hairs. I timed the perfect swipe to gash my opponent across the chest, but he made an unexpected move, he had stopped completely second s from where I slashed. My sickle missed and was caught by the skeletal staff. He wrapped the bones around it and pulled me towards him. He laughed for no apparent reason as he threw a bundle of black dust into my face and released me face first into the sand.

When I rose I was no longer in the arena. Instead I was in a graveyard of sorts. Fog and tombstones littered the yard and a bony reaper with glowing red eyes stood on the large stone ahead of me, he cackled as he clacked his bones in the air. Decomposed hands broke through the earth in a cliché fashion; it was terrifying despite the unholy fakeness with which they rose. I simply cut down the first few waves of monsters but they were persistent. I decided to pursue Epoch but he would simply go to the next tombstone and force me to run through the ghouls again to get close enough for a futile strike.

I could not stand the mere monotony of it, he hopped, a zombie flopped, and a new tombstone popped into existence. It was so long and boring, he was untouchable. I dwelled on the monotony of it until my mind had gone numb and it was at this point that I realized that each of the undead were identical as well as each epitaph. I was certain that this was one of his tricks. With this knowledge I could see beyond the false land. The reaper faded and the scrawny opponent was visible. The undead were phantoms now and I easily walked through them and caught him by surprise punching his trachea. My opponent was grasping his throat as he fell to the ground defeated.

After the match I was teleported to the field again, this time it was Djonie who had called me. He was a deep red and constantly twisting his beard. He had the voice of an angry CEO as he spoke, "why did you cheat?"

"Cheat?" I replied in an incredibly oblivious tone.

"You had someone sneak into my files through a computer feed and change the match-ups."

"You were going to make me fight a ridiculous amount of opponents! My buddy had to do something, we think you might be trying to kill me," I smiled but my voice remained serious.

"Of course I'm trying to kill you!" he roared, "you are the villain, I want you to die! You are the whole reason that I had a shot like this, it was the only condition!"

"That I die?" I asked.

"Yes," he said, "well I've said too much already, just tell me who it was that helped you."

"No," he was a flaming red after I replied.

"Well, I'll figure it out, this is going to be one interesting week don't you think?" he snapped his fingers and I was back in front of my apartment, the food encrusted door had cracked and I could now enter. Inside I found that it had been mutilated. The open window had allowed the elements to take their toll on the room, the thought of using my window to get in hadn't occurred to me. I was glad that I could still go to the cloud.

I was happily aboard and greeted by Pearl, we unfortunately were not alone as Ann and Orly had brought a small banquet for no particular reason. At one point Orly leaned over to me from his seat and whispered, "Do you remember that cold wind that blew you and Pearl together?"

"Yeah, how'd you know about that?"

"Who do you think put the air-con full blast?" the two of us laughed silently and I sincerely thanked him before we went back to our rooms, before I parted ways with Orly he told me, "when you get to your bunk be prepared for company, don't go to sleep until you here a knock on the door," he gave me a wink before dashing off.

That night a storm began to rock the cloud angrily, Orly had to land it apparently as I saw the forest through my circular window. I heard a knock on my door. It was Pearl, she needed somewhere to sleep because her window was broken, for some "unknown" reason the emergency walls failed to close against the storm and she couldn't sleep. I quickly said yes but attempted to restrain my excitement. I informed her that I only had one bed but that I would happily share with her.

I couldn't sleep now, I looked over her shoulder at her face, and she was wide awake. I let out a subtle sigh, "hey, you awake?"

"Yes," she replied.

"You wanna do something?"

She sat up quickly, "Like what?"

I paused and wondered, "I'm not sure, maybe checkers?" She nodded and I reached under the bed and pulled out a set. We played checkers beneath the covers for awhile before she grew tired of it. I saw her looking back at me as the lightning cracked nearby filling our room with white light that mixed with the blue lamp to form periwinkle overcast.

Eventually we were once again lying down but still not sleeping, instead I was overcome with a surge of desire and rotated my face to match hers. I mirrored her, her eyes glimmered with expectation, her breath was on my nose, and a smile crept over her slightly ajar mouth.

I breathed in her breath and kissed her. It was long and clumsy, then I had my second, it was better. My third excursion brought me closer into her as I felt our tongue's dance; I hadn't a clue what I was doing but soon understood my role in this exchange. I had consecutive kisses after that but the festivities were cut short by a knock on the door. Ann was wide-eyed and afraid, "Something terrible happened to Orly and I can't find Pearl!" Pearl poked her head from the semi-darkness of my room into the hall light. Ann paused, "Why are you in his room? And why are you," she took a step back, "wow. I can't believe you two!" she scolded.

"What's wrong with Orly?" I asked as I grabbed my sickle.

"He's dead." Ann flatly replied.

I ran out of my room to see my fallen comrade. He had been neatly torn open by something and every organ had been meticulously removed, but it was a clean murder. There wasn't a drop of blood, he had been completely exsanguinated. I looked around the husk and saw that his body was inside of a hexagon, at each vertex of the hexagon there were of seven holes in the steel floor arranged into a heptagon.

More holes existed a few meters from the initial hexagon. Each was the same design and shape, so I deduced that it was the tracks of whatever killed him. I began to chase down these tracks hoping to find the perpetrator. I continued my search through the rain as I exited the cloud and searched the pitch black woods. I soon had become disoriented before I lost the trail and became lost. After a long and strenuous trek through the dark labyrinth I saw Bianca. She was lying down on a tree stump without anyone around, I called out her name and she turned to see me. She grinned and jumped off the log and ran away. I ran after her, she had a dim white glow that led me through the shadows, deeper into the shadows. I soon collapsed in the misty rainforest.

A jack-in-the-box gently played a familiar tune, I walked over to it, it opened releasing a set of jaws that completely swallowed me, I spent a great deal of time in the darkness.

I awoke on a cold stone tablet of some kind. My head throbbed with a terrible pain as I stumbled over my feet. My legs refused to function properly in the rapidly spinning room. The lack of features on the wood walls only made it harder to focus. But from what I could see I was inside of a hollow tree, complete with the lack of much to see. I still could feel the ominous presence of someone else.

The only source of light was a large hole in the roof of the tree. I immediately recognized the outline of Bianca as she emerged from the shadows. I suddenly realized I was covered in mud.

Bianca didn't seem to notice my unpleasant state as she spoke in her extremely unique voice, "I want to help you win the tournament; Djonie must not succeed in his evil plans."

I paused, overjoyed, "So you want me to beat the Unstrung Aero? Isn't he your boyfriend or something?"

I saw her pristine face shimmer like a disturbed puddle. She pulled back her hair and the illusion broke. She had a stern face with less than extraordinary features. She nodded and her feet melted away into a wispy tail and the rest of her skin gained a pale green hue, "My name is Mishrel," she began in Bianca's voice, "I am Djonie's sister, not that promiscuous human you vie for. Djonie is not your genie, you did not release him."

"But I squirted that perfume bottle."

Her voice was now deeper and gained a sharper, more malignant, tone, "You humans can't be that gullible, genies come out of lamps not bottles. Anyways, his true owner is an extra dimensional spirit known as Wizadro. He knows many things and aims to destroy you; it was his only wish that you meet a quick defeat."

"Wizadro? Why would he want me dead, what did I do? I've never even met the guy."

"Nothing, but the other yous from the parallel dimensions to ours were able to defeat Wizadro. He constantly complains about the you that started his first fall. He called you the Traveler. Apparently every dimension has the same basic people in it, but their lives are adversely different, some that may be kind here are criminals elsewhere. We may not even share the same face with our copies; we are connected to them through the soul within our bodies."

My head had begun to spin again; if I had been reading this book I would reread this page about three times. I continued to listen to her story, "The Wizadro copies were sometimes insane, some were dead, some had yet to exist, but they had the same seed within them. It was their destiny to be villains, and you were destined to defeat them. That is why Wizadro wants you dead; if he can kill you he will be unstoppable. He'll also possess the champion's body since he doesn't have one. He needs a body to inhabit in order to stay anchored to this dimension. It has something to do with gravitons."

"So Djonie isn't my genie?"

I exhaled a held breath, she continued, "It's up to you to save the world. Wizadro had three wishes, the first was that he could kill you, but that is against the rules, as a result he needed to create an event that would lead to your demise, this tournament is that event. The other wishes were used to manipulate you into death."

Not exactly keeping up with the conversation I quickly asked, "Wait, in any of those worlds do I get the girl?"

She laughed before snapping her fingers and sending me to the door of the cloud in a puff of smoke. I wandered the cloud, I had no idea how long I'd been gone, but it mustn't have been too long because after around a minute of sadly sitting in the pilot seat the screen sprang to life:

ROUND 249
RED REAPER
VS.
MR. M

The familiar teleportation to the arena, the crowd of numerous alien species cheering, the bright light of the gates rising, how could I have gotten used to this? I stepped out into the sun light and was greeted with hisses and boos from the audience. Mr. M entered on his side; from this distance it was obvious that it was Rob. He was dressed in an overzealous military uniform complete with decorative golden shoulder pads and adorned with silver medals. He held a large twisted sword; it appeared to have been gnarled by a beast of some sort that bent it at every possible angle. I stepped closer I saw that his face was marred by a large scar that spread across his face.

He charged me with his tattered sword, bellowing an unnatural roar. I was chilled frozen by his murderous attack but was petrified by what I saw in his eyes. One eye was a milky blue; it showed no recognition of an actual world. His other eye had a darkness to it. Beneath the shadow that cloaked his "good" eye a deep purple flame seemed to radiate out and towards me. I broke from my trance as Ann cheered for me above the villainous cheers from the crowd. I moved away from the death blow M had prepared for me.

My opponent immediately pulled out his revolver and slowly aimed it directly at me. I was frozen by his dark eye once again. This time I felt myself recede into my mind, I remembered my friends, I realized that life had been relatively great. But that I had dwelled on that which was unimportant, I had been so consumed with my lust for Bianca. It was the one thing I so foolishly desired and Djonie took advantage of this fact, twisted and exploited my darkest hopes. It would all be ended soon; I just needed to dodge a few bullets.

The revolver rang through the arena, crowd, and surrounding areas; my sickle vibrated and released its own metallic call as it collided with my opponents attack. Rob had changed little beside his appearance, he was still undoubtedly stronger than I was but I was inherently faster and smarter. With a few more dodges of his blade and revolver I came face to face with my opponent and struck him down, in the last moment before his defeat I saw his dark eye change. For a split second it had returned to its natural brown before receding into his eyelids as he hit the dirt and was supposedly brought back to the Home-pod.

Although I had defeated Mr. M the semifinals would pit me against the Unstrung Aero. I really disliked him for all of the obvious reasons, but I couldn't help but fear his skill. It would be my hardest challenge. I knew I couldn't face him as I was and win. Apparently so did Pearl and Ann. The two of them tracked me down and voiced their concern for my life.

They already had a plan, over the next three days before the match I would have to train day and night for the match against the Aero. The only catch was I would have to spend nights in the cloud in each of their rooms to stop me from breaking any of their rules. I thought it was silly and agreed to their terms.

CHAPTER 5

Aero

I was supposed to spend the first night with Pearl and was happy to do so, but I was surprised by the formality, she forced me to sleep on the floor despite the comforting size of her bed. I placed my head on the cold floor trying to figure out what I had done wrong.

She bid me good night and slid into her bed. The thought of Pearl alone in that bed gave me an incredibly hard time sleeping. My eyes could not shut from the thoughts overflowing in my head. I soon fell into an exhausted slumber.

I'm falling. I'm falling very fast. I see no end to the shadowy pit and I am accelerating at extreme rates. I continue to fall until I begin to see light near the bottom of this pit. It illuminates and nearly blinds me and I feel warm. To my sides I see branches lodged into the stone walls, but I am moving to fast to even try and reach out to them. I am now very hot as the white ball of molten substance is only a few kilometers above me, my rapid speed brings me ever closer to the ball and just as I reach its blistering surface I feel droplets of rain on my back. All around me steam fills the room as ancient flame and nascent water collide. My bones crunch against an iron ball before I awake.

I awoke with my nose crunched against the floor. I could hear Pearl in the shower and I resisted the urge to bid her good morning at that moment. She emerged from the steamy restroom prepared for breakfast. She wore a maroon shirt and blue jeans; she took my moment of awe away as she grinned, "Don't you get tired of the same old suit?"

"Well, I thought it was a pretty neat costume, besides I have one for each day of the week so I always have a clean suit."

"Take it off," she commanded.

I obliged and stood in my shorts and shoes as I lost my hooded tunic, "now what?" I tried not to sound hopeful. She then told me to take off my sneakers as she opened a nearby closet that housed an expansive cavern full of varying clothing. Ann chose this moment to come in, she found my befuddled appearance humorous and giggled.

"Did you already tell him he needed to shave?" Ann whispered loudly to Pearl. I rubbed my chin and felt the uneven growth of a beard; my mustache must've suffered similar treatment. I dashed to the restroom immediately to see my monstrously unkempt face. I could still see the healing scars that the spider monkey had inflicted peppering my face. I used my sickle to carefully clean and groom my chin and upper lip. I left a strong and even mustache but cleared the majority of the beard allowing my sideburns to grow.

Ann cut my hair to a manageable length as pearl began to search for various outfits for me to use. I found many of them quite dull, but the three of us finally agreed on a collage of articles for my new look. It consisted of an interesting (old) black fedora hat, a comfortable (oversized) brown overcoat made of velvet, and my bright red gloves. From beneath the hat a series of curls shyly peeked out, I felt the entire get up worked well together, even my glasses. Ann then gave me a pair of blue jeans while pearl supplied me with brown flat soled sneakers that wrapped snugly around my feet. She called them moon boots which only increased my joy to have them.

I happily plunged my fork into one of Ann's cakes as the make over was completed but my utensil crashed into the marble table. Ann gave me a stern look, "do you want to die?"

"Not really," I smirked as I reached for my slice.

She slapped my hand away, "in that case you'll eat this instead," she held up a tragically green salad. She then took a bite of her angelic devil's food cake.

Between mouthfuls Pearl added, "Eat as much as you can, we'll be starting your training." Sure enough the training began. But it wasn't so much training as it was physical torture. I had no breaks of any kind, it was brutal. The "warm-up" consisted of me having to pull myself up a two meter high ledge and jump off to repeat the process; afterwards I had to do the same with my legs, which was oddly easier. Before the training had actually started Ann had supplied me with a t-shirt and extra short shorts she had hand picked for me. The two brutal coaches led me to an abandoned track afterwards.

Much like my beard had been it had the path was unkempt, uneven, and completely inhospitable. Pearl then instructed me to carry Ann on my back and do three laps, which needless to say quite literally brought me to my knees. Don't get me wrong, she wasn't fat or anything, far from it, but her hips were quite wide and, though moderately alluring, very heavy. What began as a brisk walk ended as I dragged myself and my load to the end of my third lap, slowly clawing my way to the end.

The sky was probably dark but I could not tell as my face was still ground into the broken concrete. She dismounted and seemed pleased with herself. She handed me a towel which I applied to my hot, sticky, dripping face. I discovered that I was bleeding profusely again. She apologized for "busting my face" as she put it, joking that it was an improvement. Pearl had already left the two of us while I had been "Training."

I entered Ann's room and was surprised by its hospitable scent. It smelled like chicken. She bandaged my face again while we waited for the chicken to finish cooking. When it had at last finished she pulled it out, broiled to perfection and sprinkled with spices. I readily devoured the preapproved bird as we discussed the plans for the next match.

I began the conversation with the simple question, "How am I supposed to survive? No one has ever lasted more then two seconds with the Aero."

"You just have to work on your agility," she replied simply.

I paused for a moment as I rolled the bit of chicken in my mouth around and thought of a reply, "in case you haven't noticed, I've a wide build; therefore I'm an easy target even with my relatively quick speed."

"Fine then," she said as she finished her small meal, "we'll just have to think up another strategy. She then bid me goodnight and retired to her quarters and I lay on the low mattress that I was given. I remained awake for a long time before finally slipping away again.

The stars above me were beautiful; every shade of every color, even a few tints. They were also very bright, illuminating the barren stone slab I stood on. I looked over the edge and saw that the slab stretched down into the abyss below; as I look out to the distance I can see the pagoda from before shining bright red and devoid of fog. A mist lies below it, no doubt from the colliding molecules of water emptying from it.

I nearly tripped on the perfectly smooth surface as I leaned toward the edge. I saw that the slab was now growing from its base and forming a pyramid. I somewhat unwisely decide to slide down the pyramid to investigate the dark reaches, I feel no fear. At the bottom I find three skeletons. The first is a remarkable dragon with its claws held up to the dark sky above me, it has a small smoldering flame within its skull that allowed me to see the dark bones.

The other pile of bones belonged to spherical creature lacking much more than a large jaw and small limbs. Both the dragon and this sphere were illuminated greatly by the fresh pile of bones which was burning brightly. The skeleton was that of a human, his organs popped grossly as I heard the crack of hair burn. The body had a tattered red tunic on it. A face of terror was chiseled onto its skull. It began to convulse and scream violently.

I was awoken by a small round object lodged into my side, "wake up, I got an idea!" Ann was ecstatic.

"Oh goodie," I moaned as I slipped out of my low lying bed onto the floor, "what is it?"

"Try to dodge this," she said as she threw another sphere, this one crashed into my face, "in order to be a true warrior you'll need the reflexes required, throughout the day I'll throw these balls at you and you have to dodge them."

I was pelted with orbs all day, even Pearl joined in on it. They never relented, as I walked, as I ate, as I continued training. My body quickly went numb and bruised, and I was horrifyingly annoyed. I soon blocked an assailing orb and immediately dodged another. The pace quickened but I was invincible, it seemed to actually be working. I had become an agile ghost unable to be struck by any object.

At the end of the day I walked with Pearl to her room. She politely asked me to wait outside. After a thirty minute wait she allowed me to open the door and asked me what I thought. The room had somehow been expanded and a series of obstacles were laid out in front of me. She was in her bed at the end of the course. She then said, "We already know you are a true warrior but is your heart true enough for this task?"

The first obstacle was a flat track of burning coals; she commanded me to remove my shoes before I could go across. I did so and focused on Pearl as my feet were scorched by the stones. I was across and now had to dodge five pendulums parallel to each other swinging at varied paces. I continued to focus as hard as I could on pearl's face as I rolled past the large blades and eventually made it to a slippery ramp. As I stumbled up the ramp quickly I soon realized that I would have to this calmly and with a considerably lower heart rate, so I thought of Ann. I patiently and carefully slid up the ramp and reached the top, unfortunately my every step was steeped in whatever oil Pearl had laid on the ramp so the next part would be extremely difficult.

Ahead of me were a series of pillars which I would have to jump onto in order to reach the next part. I focused on Mishrel as I hopped across each one maintaining my balance. I had reached the last pillar and was preparing to jump when Bianca's face interrupted my concentration. I immediately stumbled and fell off of the pillar and was sent back to the slippery slope. I continued my trek and eventually finished the pillar challenge. Next was a room that had a series of arrows being shot from various angles at the center path. Focusing on Ann once again I anticipated each bolt and made it across with relative ease. Ahead of me was a series of spinning blades that led to the ground once again. I thought of the mysterious Mishrel and was able to find footing on the speedy blade and reached the ground. I knew that only one obstacle lay before me. A large wall of varying material was ahead of me. Ann's calm did not help, Pearl's speed was of no use, and Mishrel's balance was irrelevant to demolishing a door. I finally indulged my longing and thought of Bianca. I thought of her every feature; from her rainbow eyes to her silk hair, from her voluptuous lips to her voracious curves. I plowed into the wall with unstoppable angst as my thoughts suddenly turned to her lover, the Unstrung Aero. I ripped into the wall without fail. I did not pause as I demolished the wall for the Unstrung Aero's visage taunted me. When the dust had settled and I stepped over the rubble I looked into Pearl's frightened eyes and had a realization, my heart had yet to be true, the turmoil within me tugged at every end of it, I was not yet at peace. I took another look at Pearl, her eyes never leaving me, nor mine hers. I walked away back through the course and left the room, throwing away a nice warm bed. As I walked in the darkness my mind whipped back and forth within in my skull, I had suddenly come to a deadly conclusion, I was going to die. I knew that Djonie had to be lying, he would ensure my death. I stopped at a tree and emptied out my gut of bile and food.

The sudden expulsion helped to remove the fog over my brain. Perhaps the cuisine had created the blood lust in every warrior? I shook my head as I pushed away the new fear, I suddenly became unbearably dizzy. I panted against the tree as I attempted to prioritize my thoughts. Ann and Pearl were my friends, nothing more; I repeated this to myself aloud for as long as I could, as soon as I was sure I had convinced myself of this I began to think of Bianca. I couldn't bring myself to speak. I slumped onto another tree as I fell into an exhausted slumber.

I'm lost and I'm alone again. The sky is devoid of light yet the ground is bright and pale. A red bolt of lightning tears through the sky followed by two others. Their roar is deafening, a mockery of true sound, ripping the air around me and igniting the earth beneath me. I begin to burn away as the green flames lick my flesh, the meat falling from glistening bone as the fat pops in a sickly fashion.

My bones are all that remain though they tenaciously stand tall, I walk across the land ablaze toward an object in the distance, the scene is silent other then the lively fire and clack of bone onto stone. My hollow eyes behold a temple of marble draped in soft yellow sheets hanging from rafters. My senseless bones do not feel the soft caress of the drapes. But I am now lost within the structure as the fluff has fogged my path, and they proceed to wrap around me, the grip tightens and I feel myself swaying a distance above the wooden floor I had recently stood upon. I bump into something in the rafters; I see that it is a body.

Beyond it are more, their faces are each concealed as the drapes completely consumed the skull and left the body to hang over the terrifying abyss. Another body holds my scythe in a shriveled hand. I take hold of it and begin to thrash about with my blade, slicing the silk and linen prison. As I gain movement and attempt my escape on the odd silk road the hung bodies burst to un-death and pursue me. There decayed hands clawing to my bones, ripping me apart bit by bit. My shattered body releases my weapon and the monstrosities cease their grip. And I fall, I plummet further and further until the abyss brightens and I am suddenly flying upwards. The temple is far behind me and I am hurtling towards the peaks of very bleak mountains. Within the crater atop a particular mountain a caldera of flame is distinctly visible. My descent into this fiery lake slows as I see a small balcony several meters above the pit of lava.

Bianca stands smiling with her own power, all around her is blood red yet she maintains the beautiful white aura that floats around her. Within her eyes I see a lack of glamour. Her eyes are more like coals then the marble slate that they represent. A thin and cruel smile spreads across her immaculate face. Her gracious arm is hooked beneath that of the Unstrung Aero, he is a terror to behold, not due to a horrific appearance, but because we have an understanding. We understand that he will kill me, and we both know he will enjoy it.

The sun shone brightly through the tree I had passed out under. I felt terrible, my gut was twisted, and my hair dripped with sweat while plastered to my brow. I wasn't even suited up for the days match. Ann and Pearl found me beneath the tree and immediately began to bombard me with questions. I hadn't thought out my actions the night before very well. My hash browns stayed untouched as I feared for my life. I could feel him watching me, laughing. I jerked my head from side to side but he was nowhere to be found. Ann was preoccupied with some other event but Pearl kindly put her hand on my shoulder. She assured me that it would be alright, "you have a true heart within you," she assured me. I turned to her and gave a queasy smile. The fear pierced her eyes as well. I wouldn't be winning. We solemnly stared at the monitor as it lit up with my sentence:

ROUND 253
UNSTRUNG AERO
VS.
RED REAPER

From within my cramped compartment I could hear the crowd cheering. My death was the best show in the realm. It was a full house. Bits of dust fell from the ceiling onto my hooded head. I stepped out into the boos and hisses of the crowd. Perspiration avalanched off of my face. Each droplet turned to salt before it could hit the searing sand. My red cloak had been stained with pink stripes where my excessive sweat had washed the tint away and the handle of my sickle was lubricated requiring an extra firm grip. I panted beneath the suit; my chest heaving to contain the thin air still available to me. I watched his gate slowly open. I stared into the blackness; I immediately ducked as the glimmer of a fired arrow tore the shadows towards me. The crowd gasps but I pay them no mind focusing on the darkness. I felt my eyes burn with great ferocity as sweat oozes onto my corneas. I close my eyes to blink away the sting. The air is cut by a twang; I feel something pierce my skin. I feel my blood spill onto the field. I was defeated.

CHAPTER 6

Russo

If you've ever died, which hopefully you haven't, you'd know how queer it feels to experience the shift. Since before birth you exist, you have a soul and a body. You are constantly tethered to your body, you eat, you sleep, you live. But death changes all of that; you are cut, released from your body and allowed a few moments of reflection. While I lied there gasping for dwindling life I looked back at my life. I watched the humiliating struggle to gain the affection of a girl who wanted nothing of me. Then I pondered, what am I doing? I just died for her and she won't care at all. She'll only know that the Aero won. I obviously could not stand (or fall) to see my story fade away and be replaced with the heroic Aero's unrivaled victory.

My sight has left me by this point as well as every other sense, the muffled roar of the crowd has thankfully ceased, and I suddenly felt aware of only myself. The void consists entirely of my miniscule essence. But my soul was restless. I was destined for victory; I couldn't allow myself to die, not yet. I decided to will myself to life or stay dead trying. I focused all of my fury into revival, anger towards Djonie, detest towards myself, hatred towards Aero, Scorn towards Bianca, and outrage towards a fool's blind love. I knew my purpose now. I was meant to win, I was meant to vanquish, there was no room in my soul for love, it was merely a hindrance. Rage would be my only companion. Rage and Justice. Djonie would pay, Aero would pay, and Bianca would see.

My heart beat was barely audible but it had once again begun, and it was undeniably true. I burst from my comatose state and was greeted by an even deeper darkness. My muscles were stiff, my eyes strained against the perpetual shadow, but at least I could feel again. The air was tight around me and wreaked of decay, I felt as if I was in a coffin. My mouth was tainted with formaldehyde.

As I rocked my wood prison back and forth musty dust drifted into my lungs, hindering my breathing. The box shattered and I rolled onto my back coughing vehemently. The catacombs around me were a foreboding network of caves lined with an unnatural amount of similar caskets, most with crushed covers revealing shriveled bodies in various costumes. I now knew the true destination of Djonie's victims. My sickening revelation was cut short as a terrible wailing resonated throughout the caverns and pale blue light flooded my view. White tendrils slithered through the air and smashed into closed sarcophagi rending flesh and bone, wood and stone, alike.

Shrapnel littered the immediate area. The ghostly arms were *eating* the dead heroes, even Rob was among the decimated. I bravely cowered in a corner as the apparitions sped passed me. The phantoms finished their fearful feast after an hour or so and left an uneasy silence in their wake. I followed the dissipating lights throughout the tomb until I found their source. A small perfume bottle sat on a stone pedestal. I fearfully lifted the bottle and smashed what I hoped was Djonie's tether to the tangible world. A strange and alarming nausea assaulted me as an unseen force washed over me and throughout the cavern of souls.

A bright and glistening hole of hope pierced the heart of darkness ahead of me. I was in awe of the beauty before me. Despite my understanding that such amorous feelings would only bring me pain I could not withstand her beauty. I saw first her angular nose, then her voluptuous hair, then her unobtainable flower. We were now face to face. I tripped over a discarded bone and scuffed my knee. I lifted myself from the unbearably cold earth and looked into Bianca's blazing hazel eyes.

She led me through the doorway into a ballroom. She walked passed the elaborate pearl structures laced with gold and beckoned me to a garden of chrome flowers. She was silent until I had reached its center; "Stay here," her voice rang out like the trumpets of a thousand angels.

"What? What do I do?" I puffed.

She tossed me my sickle and gave me a wink and smirked, "You'll figure it out." She may have been an illusion, I suppose, but the message was certainly sincere. I watched as all around me the beautiful scenery melted away and was replaced by a pit of sand. Suspended and walled by chains. To my left was the Unstrung Aero, his immaculate attire an unearthly green. To my right was the Blue Brawler whom was lovingly polishing his cleaver. He was entirely covered in bulky blue armor his own blue cloak was poking out through small creases at his joints. The Aero's eyes widened as he beheld me, as though I was a ghost to him.

Djonie' floated overhead speaking out to the crowd, which were suspended on all sides of the arena including directly above the cage we stood in. Djonie blathered on about a free wish to the victor of the match and introduced each of us. I instinctively dodged Aero's first volley which were sent at me the instant the djinn had disappeared. The Blue Brawler charged me blindly his azure armor glistened and sparkled as arrows broke and bounced away. I simply side stepped the blue brute, his laborious blade slinging sluggishly through the air. I struck my sickle against his spine with incredible precision. The resonating impact jarred my chin and I felt a tooth chip as a hearty laughed erupted from the hulking villain.

Not even a scratch.

Aero continued a seemingly endless assault with his arrows and would have surely skewered me had I not used the Brawler's own armor as protection by keeping his back to the antagonistic archer. Using Blue as a shield I fled Aero's range in order to face my bulky opponent on even grounds, or so I thought.

The brutal battle lasted longer than I had expected due to the fact that he was exceptionally fast. As I struck at each exposed joint he would merely shift his position and deflect my weapon away, one clever move sent my sickle flying from my hands to the edge of the stage. Aero was closing in from afar, Blue was tireless too, I was exhausted. But I did not relent. I dodged each of his crushing blows catapulting sand over me. And there I was. Covered in sand, caked in sweat, staring at an evil doppelganger with bad hair, holding an unimaginably large cleaver-like sword. I was doomed.

Again.

Death laughed at me from the glint of his misshapen blade. Just as he raised his weapon a strange thing happened. I looked up. Up past the Brawler, past the cage, into the inverted stands, Ann was in despair, gritting her teeth and wringing her hands. The bow in her hair wiggled as the wind nudged it ever so slightly; it fell off her head with a small gust. She caught the bow but the sharp pin holding it in tumbled down and landed on my chest. I thrust the pin up in a futile attempt to stop him and was relieved when I heard the thump of his blade against sand as opposed to my skull.

I opened my tightly squeezed eyes and saw Blue holding his throat, a trickle of blood coming from both sides of his mouth and from between his fingers. His eyes rolled back in his head and he fell to the ground writhing from the ridiculous wound. The pin in my hand was drenched in blood. An arrow struck the sand beside me, it was a warning, Aero wanted to play. I ripped off two bits of my clone's armor to use as shields. I lugged the plates around me sluggishly spinning them so as to deflect my opponent's volley.

Once he was a mere meter away I swung the two blue chunks of armor down in a murderous blow. The sand crunched under the brutal force. Aero snickered and I felt sand enter my eyes. The cackling continued, "You are weak, you are blind, you are slow. Why do you refuse to give up?"

I gritted my teeth, "Because I am meant to win, you are a puppet to that smoky sultan, Djonie!"

I heard Aero scoff, and then a sharp and melodic twang. I ducked and felt wind tear past the top of my head, "So, you dodged the first one without your sight. You can't win, even if you are a true warrior. Djonie!"

I heard a benign pop as Djonie appeared, "Yes, Mr. Aero?" he said in a deceptively servile tone.

"Restore his sight, and leave me only three arrows. I wish to finish him of my own accord, without your magic."

"Are you mad? He dodged your arrow without even seeing you!" Djonie gasped.

"I wasn't even trying, now do as I say or I'll personally skewer you with my blade," I had no idea that he had a sword, "don't question me genie understand?" He was unnaturally calm.

Djonie grumbled a weak protest as he snapped his fingers and I regained my vision. Soon after Aero began to insult me out loud for the crowd to hear, "Come now, you coward! Face me and meet your doom," he glanced back and smiled at Bianca, whom was giggling.

"I've met Doom before!" I replied from across the field, "he's quite nice, we sort of have a deal, I help his buddy Death with some of his marks and he comes to visit me but never in malice," I gave a grim smile to him, "the two are near, can't you hear them?" I held a hand to my ear as if listening, "can't you hear death's song?"

My taunts had unsettled Aero, "Y-you are mad," he spat, "I will make quick work of you!" He fired his first shot at my heart. I ducked in such a manner that I nearly fell on my back and the tip of my chin was nicked by the bolt. He grunted as he saw that I was in fact still alive.

The roar of the crowd paused for half a second as they were as shocked as my opponent. I thought I heard Ann say, "He is a true warrior, and he has a true heart," but I couldn't be sure. The next dart was released aimed at my chest again. I jerked my body in an unnatural twist that popped every bit of my vertebrae and sent a sharp pain into my sides. He yelled as he came upon the realization that I could defeat him.

His final shot was as silent as the wind through the trees and I barely noticed it as it sped toward my sternum. And it would have struck had I not put my hands in front of it. I felt the rending of thin flesh and glove as the tip punctured first my left hand. It traveled through multiple layers of muscle and bone until it exited and drove into my right hand. At this point I realized that besides the excessive blood spattering against my face my two hands could not completely slow the shaft. It was at this moment that I remembered my purpose. I was meant to win. I wrapped my still tearing hands around the projectile and grabbed hold. The hands were less than functioning but they did the job needed.

The arrow tore threw the fabric of my cloak and pricked my chest. I looked up, the crowd was silent, every one of them was wide eyed as their hero failed to kill me. My purpose might not have been that good, but it was true. Aero was nowhere to be seen. Had I won? Had my unspeakable survival scared him away to whatever lavish hole he calls home?

My answer came with the crunch of sand behind me. I swung my fist remembering that I had yet to retrieve my weapon. Aero gave a hearty chuckle, "Ooh, bravo, bravo! You managed to survive quite some time, but you're nothing more than a rat. A rat clinging to a sinking ship and somehow have survived by stepping on the biggest of your ilk. Now you shall be the first to taste my blade," he reached behind himself and pulled out a beautifully sculpted sword.

Its golden hilt seemed to glitter from an infinite amount of points, a blinding sheen similar to that of staring at the sun. The blade was that of what I believed to be copper, due to its sea green hue. Throughout the blade itself were veins of emerald that pulsated with what would seem to be their own life force. The overall appearance reminded me of the first days of autumn, when the tip is golden but the rest of the leaf is as lively as ever.

The unstrung Aero handled the ornate weapon with ease plowing through the sand with each individual stroke. I could hardly escape the windmill attacks that were being tossed at me. Desperation closed in again, it seemed that I was making a habit of being doomed. His prowess made my demise inevitable unless I could figure out some way to beat him. Death by this royal blade would be almost dignified, I thought. I mulled the thought around in my skull as the Aero continued his calm slices at my soul and I haphazardly evaded each blow coming closer and closer to the edge of the ring.

Accepting death as a friend as I had said before I charged my opponent, he happily raised his blade with all his might believing me to put myself at his mercy. As he plunged his blade down across the length of my body I rolled away. His blade fell full force upon the blade of my sickle, denting my blade by ninety degrees. Aero's blade did not fare as well. The primal impact shattered the jewels and metal of his blade, fragments of precious gem peppered his limbs and face, he screamed in agony as every blink of his eyes drove the stones deeper into his corneas. I walked over to his screaming, squirming body; I kicked away what remained of his blade and kneeled over his mutilated face.

"This isn't possible!" he wailed, "Djonie told me that I was destined to win, I saw it with my own eyes!" the blood oozed from his gashes onto the sand. I felt a sickening pleasure at seeing his suffering. His back arched in pain, the gems seemed to be burrowing further on their own accord. Closer inspection of his broken sword revealed that each fragment was in fact enchanted to reassemble. So I decided to grab the blade. I helped Aero stand up and jabbed the base of his spine with the blade, flames of pain nearly caused him to faint. I looked into his pathetic eyes. The primal fear in his eyes was both empowering and accusing. It was pitiful. It seemed that he was crying but I could not tell past his various wounds. I held the blade over his arms first; the shards agonizingly released themselves from his flesh. He remained immobile besides the now evident sobbing and shivering. The crowd was entirely silent, not a cheer could be heard.

The lack of cries of pain alarmed me and I looked at the butchered face, he was passing out. I yelled out, "Aero!" his eyes fluttered open, "try to stay alive okay? Just try to speak."

"I'll try," he replied through gritted teeth.

"Now," I began, "what is your real name?" he yelled out something inaudible as his pain reached a high point, the blade was directly over his face, "stay with me Aero, just stay awake, it's almost over. Next question how is Bianca?"

A smug smile cracked his decimated face, "she is so awesome, we had decided that after this match we were going to finally do-," I broke his sentence by waving the sword back and forth; this caused the shrapnel to dance in his face. Blood spurted up like a fountain into my face. His voice cracked with pain, "oh," he laughed, "I didn't know you liked her," he smiled, blood coated his teeth, "cute, well I hope you get a crack at her, she's a wild one," his chauvinistic smile contorted as I pressed the blade against his face, "okay, okay, I get it. You actually like her, she's a bit of a bit-," I cut him off again, his blood drenched both of us and the sand around us; it was an unnatural amount of blood. The gems had finally escaped his face but he was still in pain, more so now than ever. The blade had several chips along its edge; the pull was stronger than before.

"Aero, I need you to tell me where the pain is, come on," Aero scratched at his chest. I tore off the green leather hauberk and revealed his chest which had received numerous miniscule wounds. They had been in him too long though and I assume vital organs were already wounded. He let out his last breath before I could extract the final shard.

Djonie appeared with an audible pop as Aero's desecrated body disappeared, "the champion is none other than the Impervious Red Reaper!" he turn to me, "see? I knew you'd make it!"

"You tried to kill me, *multiple times.*"

"Kill is such a strong word, I prefer disqualified," a grim smile spread across his face, "anyways all you must do to receive your prize is think of your wish as you place your hand on this," he held out a purplish egg with a strange inscription:

I hesitantly took hold of the unbearably cold stone, the entire crowd was watching, Djonie wouldn't kill me here, would he? I wished for Bianca to love me the way I love her, I didn't mean too, it was the first thought on my mind, but then something strange happened. My fingers went numb, then my arms. Both were immobile by the time my legs began to suffer the same fate. Soon the entire range of my senses receded into my skull as I stood in a stupor. Djonie's laughed echoed in my head.

Before completely slipping away into my psyche I heard myself laugh along, a disturbing cackle, then I heard myself wish for supreme power, Djonie stopped laughing.

CHAPTER 7

Wizadro

The darkness was, as expected, extremely dark, my mind felt strangely bound. Kind of like a pillow was held over my face with a tiny hole cut in to it so I could barely breathe. Everything felt fuzzy. I willed some kind of image into my head, I needed to see something. I saw myself fettered to a floorless ground. I could not escape these chains, and I began to thrash wildly, the grinding of the cuffs against my wrists felt like blenders in my brain.

"Stop that, you'll only wear yourself out," the voice was monotone and unfamiliar.

"Who said that?" I thought.

"My name is Wizadro, I am a conjuring of your own thoughts, the ones you are unable to perceive yourself. I intend to help you; Djonie was nothing more than a figment of your imaginings. This entire ordeal was a simple nightmare."

"What?"

"You are dreaming, you are resisting your awakening, this is the basest form of your mind, this is how it looks in your head," he seemed annoyed, "it's seems quite empty in my opinion," the neutral voice shifted to a shriller pitch, "simply put your mind to rest, ignore the urge to rise and convince yourself to sleep, then you will awake," the voice took form as it oozed out of my myriad mind. It was an unsettling apparition; he was clad in maroon velvet. Wizadro wore this velvet in a cloak that enshrouded his entire body from the neck down. The stranger had a terrible face, unrealistic and cold, his iron skull had two oversized horns flanking it. Oversized eye sockets held feeble blue skin with piercing black eyes. A perpetual smile with two large fangs on the roof of the mouth was set into the metal mask. More watery skin peeked from under the maniacal grin.

Wizadro wrapped his twig thin hands around my mind's shoulders. His fingers were bony and cold as death, "just sleep, rest, I'll take it from here," I was drowsy and felt icy all over, my mind had chilled. He was chuckling to himself as I slipped into the abyss. A wave of corruption wracked my psyche and shook me from the comforting sleep. Beneath Wizadro's grinning mask I could see a grimace, "my friend," began the phantom, "why have you awoken, sleep to awaken, remember?"

There suddenly appeared a vision of me in a crumbling tower, freezing his body alongside my own to ensure his defeat. I could feel in my soul's memory that I had to make this sacrifice to end him. Yet it could not have been me in that tower, it had never happened. It wouldn't happen, but now I knew what I was facing. The memory began to fade away.

"I know what you are," I whispered, a new vague and blurry memory permeated my mind I somewhat understood what this monster was, "I remember you!" I spat, my bindings began to weaken as I grew braver.

"You can't possibly remember. You couldn't. You're not him! You're a different imbecile! You're not *my* Traveler!" Wizadro seemed to be talking to himself as opposed to me.

"Would you mind telling me exactly what's going on?" I wondered if the demented abomination would share what he knew.

"Well, since this foolish charade seems to have failed I'll simply have to kill you. No use in keeping you oblivious to the reason I'll destroy you though. I came from another plane of reality from yours. On my home-plane I had descended from a long line of powerful warlocks, most were content with dominion over a mountain range or swamp, islands too. I wanted the entire universe!" the black void shifted around us to show a beautiful mountain range, we were standing atop a black mountain balcony, "I managed to conquer a whole planet, but my imbecilic sister blew it up."

"Bummer"

"Don't interrupt!" he snapped, "Anyways, a small group of self-proclaimed 'heroes' led by an opposing wizard decided to stop me. While they fought legions of my minions and amassed an army of their own I had been researching delightful particles called gravitons.

"You see gravitons are the particles that make up gravity, unlike the forces keeping atoms and magnets together gravitons are not planarly bound. I determined that if I could harness the power of gravitons I could simply ride the particles to traverse the multiverse. But I had no need to do so, and it was still merely a theory. Then those 'heroes' came knocking on my door," the void shifted to a still frame of various monsters fighting each other, angels overhead, lizards and robots clashing, fiery beasts and fairies fought shades and ghouls. It was both terrifying and beautiful, "I felled a great deal of them but one particular imbecile got in my way. He was my Traveler, a being that seemed almost immune to death, much like you. He managed to freeze me and sink my castle Esruc into the depths of the planet we were on.

"I projected my mind outwards searching for any living being to exert my influence on, it wasn't for several centuries before I gripped the heart of a lowly pilgrim that happened by the site of my imprisonment. I had him obtain gravitons and begin my research anew. After forcing him to kill himself I began to harvest passing gravitons with a special spell I won't repeat again. The first plane I visited was inhabited by the Kyrie, they didn't take my presence kindly and their Traveler kicked me out.

"It was at this point I discovered that once you leave a plane by graviton you can't go back. I kept this in mind as I visited other planes each time attempting to rule that universe but being defeated by various Travelers. After so many failures at their hands I formed a genius scheme. Why am I fighting my weakness? Instead I've decided to possess him, use the designated protector of that universe as my vessel! So do me the favor of taking a nap."

"How old are you? Because you're obviously senile," I smirked.

"Imbecile, I tried to do it the easy way but if you refuse to sleep, I shall be obligated to use force," reaching into his robe, Wizadro pulled out a twisted black staff, set at its top was a sphere the size of a cantaloupe filled with purple clouds, "prepare to roast!" My skull filled with flame as pulses of energy reverberated from the sphere. Breaking from the brittle bonds I bounded away from the blasts of shadow.

My nightmarish assailant was relentless, a vortex of murky water formed around me. It rose as a column and began to consume my mind's avatar. As the water reached the base of my neck, I received a stroke of thought. Using the analogous effects of Wizadro willing water into existence I focused all my thought and emotion into fire. I envisioned every synapse in my mind bursting into flame. A conflagration erupted in my consciousness, boiling its contents; soon my inflating ego popped revealing an exit from my subconscious. Pulling Wizadro along with me emerged into the land of the (relatively) sane.

The entire exorcism must've only lasted a minute or two because the distance between the currently terrified audience and their abandoned seats was not nearly as far as it had seemed. I deduced that Wizadro had decided to inhabit Djonie next. This unfortunate discovery arose from an unsettling and heinous cackle behind me, or rather two simultaneous cackles meshed together.

It was as if they shared the throat yet resonated from separate vocal chords. I turned to greet my opponent; I was prepared for almost anything, almost. I had been expecting either Wizadro's demented mask or Djonie's facetious smirk. I saw a shocking splicing of the villains. Djonie composed much of the monster itself, though the body was broken, wispy. He was seemingly decomposing; bits of the murky form began to drift out into oblivion.

The striped belt he once wore was torn in two. A jagged mouth spread out of his abdomen, hungrily panting, releasing a fetid rancid smell. It seemed to beckon souls to sacrifice themselves. My skin crawled as the smaller mouth began to move in an odd fashion and a screeching scrawl of a voice slithered out of their shared throat, "You imbecile, because of what you've done two things have occurred. One, you ticked me off royally. Two, you halved my power and currently have it. Now, I have no choice but to rend your soul from its body and devour both afterwards. I'm going to enjoy this immensely."

Djonie's belt-void opened wider and began to inhale violently. The hair on my arm turned frail and powdery and drifted into the terror's maw. The grass beneath my feat had blackened considerably and I deduced that the beast's mouth was expelling a necromantic toxin as it devoured the rotted material. My blade was dulling as my ears began to burn. My eyes were unbearably dry while my lungs lost the ability to hold proper air in.

Pearl was at my side immediately, wielding an unnaturally large hammer in addition to a murderous and determined scowl. She charged the phantom and slammed its side with her mallet. Djonie exhumed a wail from his true lips and turned to her. His face was distorted and a dent persisted in his ribs. He murderously growled as another strike through him to the ground, "you imbecile!" the earth shook with his roar, "You'll be the first to go then."

I limped towards the beauty and beast locked in combat. Now that he was no longer surprised it was more of a brutal beating and Pearl didn't seem any closer to getting a third hit. I lifted my dented and dull scythe in a threatening manner, Wizadro just laughed, "imbecile," he hissed, "I can crush your very being with a thought, put down your weapon and succumb to my will; this will end your suffering sooner."

"I've got a better idea," I replied between brittle teeth as I watched Pearl wind up one last shot, "how about you just get decapitated and we call it a day?" Wizadro barely had time to turn around as she knocked his head off its shoulders, "you should've quit while you were a 'head'. You could have been 'head' of the class. At least you had a good 'head' on your shoulders," once I'd run out of puns I exhaled and observed my surroundings, the whipping winds around me began to dissipate and I saw that I was back on Earth; the library next to the orange grove, my school and the cafeteria. Djonie was dead and I was back home. I happily ran to Pearl, whom was looking out into the distance with a loose grip on her hammer, swaying slightly, side to side.

She had a contorted grin spread across her face, "you thought I'd be that easy to beat?" cackled Wizadro through her voice, "I doubt you'll kill another friend, an innocent one at that!" he nearly toppled over in demented laughter.

Several thoughts flooded my brain, but none of them involved me fighting Pearl. I bowed my head in defeat, "you're right, I can't hurt her. You win."

"Would you mind saying that again?" the body bent closer to me, "I didn't quite catch that last bit."

"I will allow you once again into my mind, but only if you let her go," the shade agreed and I commanded Pearl to run as far away as possible before I was completely overshadowed by the villain and forced back into my skull.

Unlike before when I was gently lulled into mental submission, the villain dove into my psyche, savagely and haphazardly rending my thoughts and dreams in the most literal sense possible. I lost all recollection of my fourth grade year of school as well as all teachings regarding mercy and strangely enough, the way an apple tastes.

Shackled once again, Wizadro wasted no time on diplomacy. A mental whip lashed my bare mind. His shrill laughter twisting joy into sorrow and contorting pleasure to pain, no true good went untainted by the torture. After what seemed like an eternity and a half my mental pain numbed.

Wizadro's terrible mask materialized before me, it towered over me, gargantuan and horrible. His pupil was so large I could leap through it were I not bound to the dry scaly ground, which I realized was actually his gloved hand. Wizadro showed off a toothy grin, "so, how are you feeling?"

"Better than you look," I spat, "by far." The twang of pain behind my left eye voiced his displeasure. Several vultures materialized, circled me, and then dove towards me ripping at my gut.

Wizadro petted a vulture perched on top of my skull, "being inside your mind is so much more interesting than most. Especially the story of Prometheus, of course, I agree with your idea that vultures are a bit better than eagles when it comes to torment."

I gritted my teeth as the fowl fowls nibbled at a kidney, "How long have you had control over my body?" I said as a wet pop and splash followed the piercing of my mind's stomach.

"Well, it's only been three hours but I've already set to work razing the fields around us and constructing a crystal spire that will outshine the drab Esruc of my home world."

"Is there anyone with you?"

"Not a soul," he smiled, "they're all quaking in fear kilometers away!"

"Good," I smiled despite the loss of my right eye. Before the monster could reply I willed away my carrion captors as well as the fetters binding me. My features began to heal and regenerate as I regained control of myself. I summoned a white hot sword of flame and slashed at Wizadro. He responded with his own murky blade. The phantasmal smoke drifting from each clash began to fill the confines of my mind, forming a deadly fog. The fight could have lasted centuries, in fact it might have, but soon I began to use my memories.

First, I leapt over Wizadro twisting his mask one hundred and eighty degrees, strangely enough he lived, then he tore off his mask. He removed his cloak as well revealing that his entire body was composed of a stringy black substance. His head was a wispy tear drop shape that drifted off into the void. His eyes were devilishly black and the scowl spread across his face morphed into a malicious grin. His watery head rippled as an unexpected laugh viciously resonated in my skull. His shoulders began to ooze upward forming intimidating shoulder pad like formations. His gloves ripped as shadowy claws revealed themselves. His final piece of transformation was his weapon which changed from a black blade to a flail of smoky ice.

My match with Skipper saved me from his first attack; I promptly flipped Wizadro onto his back as I had done to my first opponent before. I remembered some moon mask guy and used the same concept once the villain changed his tactics; I had to anticipate the strategy he would utilize. This went on for some time until Wizadro tapped into my memories of the Aero. Wizadro smiled as he drank in my hatred for the false hero and used it to bring himself even greater power. This was his ace.

But I had my own.

I willed into existence a dozen copies of myself, we shuffled at a rapid pace towards the demon in a blaze of heroics. His every shot met a phantasm. Wizadro burst into tears as I held a dozen flaming swords to his neck, acrid steam drifted where each acidic drop touched the blade, "By the Deus himself, why must you always defeat me? You always win!" he wailed, "Every time, every plan I make is foiled by you! Conquering Metalmorphon, stealing the jewels of Mar, creating a universe spanning empire, none of it follows through! I always lose. And it's always to you."

I allowed my duplicates to fade, I stood slightly to his right, I still held my blade to his throat, "You've no right to exist," I told him, "you are an abomination and I must destroy you."

"So, I'm going out on a limb and saying that pity doesn't affect you very well?" Wizadro sneered as the crocodile tears faded, "oh well, time for plan B," a multitude of amethyst spears burst from the shadows and skewered me in various angles. Wizadro rose from the ground and acted as though he was dusting himself off, "well it's good to know you're more gullible than most Travelers. You defeated me thirty two times before in various universes, but I finally have my own victory you imbecile!"

I gurgled out blood as I attempted to reply, I was immobile, and he continued to laugh. Wizadro revealed a twisted dagger which he used to stab me profusely, "this is for those Hunters you led, this one's for the vampire scheme! Here's another just for fun!" I was peppered and torn by my opponent's blade. Once my body was a bit more than a barely living rag doll, he allowed the purple shards to recede. He danced over my shattered body singing a variety of insulting songs.

My abysmal chances of surviving quickly dwindled as I felt his cold fingers wrap around my brain. I refused to die, the holes punctured into my psyche bled out as my shambling remains stood up in defiance.

"So you want more, you're persistent, I like that," he taunted, "how about something a little more agonizing?" he cut off my left arm in a most swift manner, the blood loss was unreal, my vision within my own mind began to fog. I was drastically close to brain death now, my weakened will my only tether, rocking gently further and further away from sanity. He continued to dismember me until I wasn't much more than a crumpled, bleeding heap in my own skull, my soul was dying.

His hollow laugh resonated with my own incoherent screams of agony; he continued to butcher me all the while. When he finished I wasn't much more than a microscopic strand. I had been reduced to the most primitive of minds; I didn't know the difference between life, death and even my name. I was defeated, so many times before I had come back after being knocked on my face. I had used all my cunning to get out of every sticky situation, but this time I couldn't do it, blind luck would've been my only savior.

Wizadro had won.

Epilogue

For once I was lucky.

Night soon followed my massacre, my body desired rest, Wizadro happily obliged. The strand of my existence just happened to drift from all the infinite reaches of my mind into Wizadro's dreams. I did not realize just how lucky I was because, as previously stated I was a sliver of a sliver of a being. It just so happened that my adversary was being wracked by a nightmare about a red clad hero. I was lucky enough to collide with the ethereal protector's form. I immediately regained my every memory and sense as my body had constructed them. It was a wondrous feeling to feel alive again, and to understand that I could just as easily not be.

My fresh avatar is fighting a hauntingly beautiful pale white vampire, she slashes and bites at me flying from all directions and attempting to ram me with her gracious horns. I see that the area around us is a harmonious ballroom littered with fallen rocks and a great deal of bodies strewn across the perfectly etched floor. The stars are fading in the sky above and the ivory demon increases the frequency of her strikes. Wizadro sat on a balcony to the far left watching the match in increasing terror as the white monster slowly begins to weaken and smoke. The sun was rising.

I kick the fallen angel into the sunlight vaporizing her in a violent burst of flame, I turn to face Wizadro. I could tell by the shock in his eye holes that I had acted unexpectedly. With blinding speed I reached out and seized Wizadro by the throat, one more surprised face was all he could spare before I threw the vampiric villain into the light.

The panoramic scene melted away as I opened my true eyes for the first time in what seemed like an eternity, Wizadro ranted in my skull, I ignored him, enjoying the new day. The warm sun rose in the distance sending golden and pure rays into the prismatic framework of Wizadro's completed castle, not a soul could be seen in sight. The air was fresh.

I listened in to my parasitic guest, "then I'll feed your remains to my grogogiles!" I didn't know what a grogogile was, but it sounded unpleasant. He continued to rave about vengeance and violence and spitting insults towards me, I thought I'd let him get the bile out of his system before I broke the news to him. His screeching voice actually made me giggle, much to his ire.

"Wizadro," I began in a commanding voice, I could feel something resonate within me, it felt golden, "I wish to propose an ultimatum to you."

"How dare you give me an ultimatum you imbecile! I am the great and powerful ruler of-"

I swiftly ended his interruption, "you are *nothing*," I growled into my own mind, "you don't have any substance of your own, and I *allow* you to speak. So, Wizadro, either you expel yourself peacefully and relinquish your power to me or I force you out myself and banish you from this plane of existence forever."

The fiend was silent for several moments, "you couldn't possibly still have enough strength to do such a thing, nor would you know the procedure. You're bluffing," he concluded.

"Am I now? In case you hadn't noticed, I killed that vampire thing thanks to your memories, I know how the other Travelers did there thing."

"Imbecile, that doesn't even make sense to me, and I'm insane," he snickered.

"Fine," I laughed, "I warned you!" seconds later an unholy wail shredded the pristine air, echoing throughout the crystalline tower. I stood in the center of the shrieking and felt the evil being purged from me. Oily smoke began to burst from my mouth, ooze from my ears, and leak from my eyes. The pitiful howling was deafening, the oil continued to roll down my body to the ground around my feet. Eventually a black puddle remained around me, it shifted and shimmered a meter in front of me.

It convulsed and began to form into a primitive and shambling being. The oil fiend had a fake smirk spread across its phantasmal face. It gurgled a sentence out that refined until it said, "you imbecilic Travelers never cease to annoy me!" the creature sprouted arms and a space began to appear between its legs. A blue head rose from the filth as the fake smile melted away, the blue drop had a terrified expression.

Once the tainted fellow finished his formation I bid him farewell and used my own sickle to create a spatial rend. It glimmered with terrifying beauty, I grabbed my opponent by the top his head and tossed the horror into oblivion. Finally free of the terror I decided that a good nap would be proper celebration for the most powerful being in the universe. I'd fix the damage he'd done in the morning.

*　*　*

I awoke in my classroom, the paper I had been taking notes on stuck to my face. Bianca was pestering the boy in front of her as the teacher droned on about atoms. The beauty's victim bore a resemblance to the Unstrung Aero. I had evidently had the most vivid dream in recorded history, but a tinge of paranoia had crept into my psyche. I turned to a fellow student and asked him where I was.

"Come on Russo, you dunce, you're in chemistry and you've been sleeping for over an hour," he rudely replied. I had spent years in the coliseum, Pearl, our feelings, my experiences, all of that had been a dream? I looked back at Bianca, beautiful as ever, but I felt nothing. The love had been drained from my heart. I had learned to live without her, a strange and empty feeling rumbled in my gut. Ann was to the right of Bianca; I had never noticed her before now. I smiled at her, and she smiled back. After class I didn't stumble over myself in an attempt to talk to Bianca, instead I approached Ann and asked her to introduce me to Pearl; perhaps I could find love elsewhere. She was more than happy to put us together. Things seemed perfect, but it may have only been the ordeal my mind fabricated.

I went to the restroom during my final class of the day; I was once again assaulted by the stenches within. The graffiti on the wall shocked me. It depicted my exploits and final victory against Wizadro. The etchings revealed what I did not know I had done. I had rewoven the fabric of time and space, healing the tear I had used to banish Wizadro. I used the last of Djonie's gift to resurrect the fallen heroes (and some villains) and created this tablet knowing I would forget my deeds.

I left the restroom on light feet. The class ended soon after, the front of my school was filled with over awed spectators. In the center of the field was a glorious sight. A crystal tower stabbed through the earth reaching out to the sun, glimmering in its flawless light.

Printed in the United States
By Bookmasters